LIGHT THE WAY HOME

NANCY L.M. RUSSELL

RAGWEED
THE ISLAND PUBLISHER

Copyright © Nancy L.M. Russell, 2000

Technical editing: Jennifer Glossop
Cover illustration: © Judy Willemsma
Printed and bound in Canada

Ragweed Press acknowledges financial support for our publishing activities from the Government of Canada through the Book Publishing Industry Development Program (BPIDP), and from the Canada Council for the Arts.

Published by:
Ragweed Press
P.O. Box 2023
Charlottetown, PEI
Canada   C1A 7N7

Canadian Cataloguing in Publication Data
Russell, Nancy L.M. (Nancy Leigh Mary), 1963-

     Light the way home

     1st ed.

     ISBN 0-921556-78-0

I. Title.

PS8585.U774L53 2000	jC813'.54	C00-950174-6
PZ7.R9157.Li 2000		

To Rob, Callum and Tristan,
who light up every day of my life.

To my family, who will always
represent "home" for me.

To Jennifer Glossop,
for challenging me as an author,
and to Louise and Sibyl,
for believing in Island writers.

And to Breda Foley and the students
at Queen Charlotte Intermediate
— the best readers
any writer could ask for.

CONTENTS

Chapter One

WHAT'S GOING ON?

*C*hristine knew something was wrong but she just didn't know what.

"I've never heard my mom and dad yelling at each other like that," she told her friends Allie and Brittany. The girls were sitting on the front steps of Alexander Graham Bell Junior High School. It was the beginning of August, and the start of the new school year was now just weeks away. The girls were still finding it hard to believe that their grade school days were over.

Brittany stretched out her long, tanned legs and leaned back on the step, soaking in the sunshine. "My parents fight every time they're in the same room together," she said. "And of course that doesn't happen very often." Brittany flipped her long blonde hair casually and readjusted her perfectly tailored white shirt and shorts. She had a tennis lesson later that morning, and her expensive racquets were strung casually on the handlebars of her top-of-the-line mountain bike.

Some of the girls at school called Brittany "Barbie" behind her back, but Christine knew that it was just because they were jealous of Brittany, who seemed to have it all. Christine knew otherwise. Even though Brittany talked nonchalantly about the way her parents fought, Christine was sure that it bothered her more than she admitted.

Allie shook her head in disagreement with Brittany's theory. "I don't think Christine's parents are like your parents, Brittany. They used to seem happy. What else could be going on?"

Christine looked at her friend gratefully. Allie was always the most practical of the three friends, much more down-to-earth than Brittany. Her dad was a lawyer, and her mother made a lot of money with her own computer consulting firm. Though they were busy, they made a point of spending time with Allie and her sister. They also kept Allie on a strict allowance and made sure that she spent some time in the community doing volunteer work at a local seniors' home.

Allie was the tallest of the three girls, with broad shoulders and muscular legs. In Grade Seven, she had been a "jock," like Christine, more than happy to walk around in a track suit and sneakers. In Grade Eight, she decided that she wanted to be artsy-looking. She wore vividly coloured shirts with black tights or a black miniskirt, always with Doc Martens. Just before graduation, she had stunned everyone by getting a nose ring and putting blonde streaks in her brown hair. Although she probably didn't even realize it herself, Allie was always trying to upstage Brittany, which was hard to do, and to get a rise out of her parents.

Christine was the most athletic of the three, at least since Allie dropped out of sports last year. Christine was a bit of a tomboy, despite her friends' attempts to interest her in makeup and clothes. She preferred a track suit or jeans and a windbreaker to the expensive outfits that Brittany was always shopping for at the local mall.

Christine had shoulder-length light brown hair and brown eyes — very average, she thought, at least in contrast to Brittany. As usual she was wearing a baggy tee-shirt, her favourite Umbro shorts and a pair of well-worn Asic runners. Christine enjoyed running and had played for the school soccer team.

The three girls had been best friends ever since Christine's family moved five years ago to their neighbourhood. Located in the north end of Toronto, the area was full of large, sprawling houses, two-car garages and expansive backyards, many with pools. The girls went to school with the children of doctors, lawyers and company executives. For the past couple of years, they had dreamed of what it was going to be like at high school. Finally, it was just a few weeks away.

"You haven't heard what your parents are talking about?" Allie asked.

Christine had noticed something mysterious a couple of weeks ago. She had come home from a swim at Brittany's and was surprised to see her dad home from work.

"What are you doing here?" she'd asked.

"Uh, the air conditioning was broken at the office," her dad answered quickly.

That same night, she heard her parents having another heated argument and wondered if the two events were connected. The next day, though, her dad left for work at his usual time, carrying his briefcase, waving a cheery farewell to Christine and her mom.

"Maybe it's just the stress of seeing their baby girl go off to high school," Brittany said, in a teasing voice. "If I see your mom at the club today, I'll be sure to ask her what's going on."

"Don't tease, Brittany. This is serious," Allie reprimanded.

"Besides, my mom hasn't gone to the club in months," Christine replied. "All of a sudden, she's not too interested in tennis, I guess."

"Don't forget that you have to sign up for tennis camp by the end of the week," Brittany said, getting up from the steps and slinging her racquets over her shoulder. "I hear that some cool guys from Grade Eleven and Twelve are going to be the instructors this year." She gave the girls a quick wave and headed down the street on her mountain bike.

"She is way too boy crazy these days," Allie said, shaking her head.

"That's our Brittany," Christine giggled. "Well, I better head home, too. It's so weird to think that we won't be back here ever again." She gave a last look at the junior high school. "On to bigger and better things. I almost wish the summer was over."

"Oh, don't say that," Allie replied. "I'm not ready for high school yet. It's going to be so hard."

"No, it's not. It's just going to be more fun," Christine insisted.

The girls left the schoolyard, rolling their bikes along beside them.

"Call me later," Allie called, as they separated at the stoplight.

As Christine cycled into the cul-de-sac where she lived, she noticed her dad's Camry in the driveway. "Air conditioning again?" she mumbled to herself as she rode her bike along the side of the house into the backyard. Her mom and dad were sitting on the back deck. Her dad was in shorts and a shirt and gave Christine a wave.

"Hey, you, where have you been? We've been waiting for you," he said in a jovial voice, though his face looked serious.

"What's going on? Aren't you supposed to be at work today? Are you on holidays?" Christine asked.

"I'm not going back to work," her father announced, looking not at Christine but at the hedge beside the deck. "I've been on, uh, leave for the last couple of months, and now I've decided that I'm not going back." He paused, and there was an uncomfortable silence as he shifted nervously in his chair. Suddenly he got up and walked to the edge of the deck.

Christine sank into a lawn chair, her stomach twisting.

"Dad is looking at some great job options and it's just a matter of which one he is going to take," Monica Miller jumped in.

Rob Miller gave a nod. "It's just temporary, Chrissie. We'll have it sorted out in no time."

"But you've been going to work every day," Christine sputtered, trying to make sense of what her parents were saying.

"I've been pretending to go to work every day," her father replied tensely. "We didn't want you to know, at least not until I knew what I would be doing next."

Christine didn't know what to say.

"What am I going to tell my friends?" she said, after a long silence.

"Don't tell them anything," her father snapped. He left the deck abruptly and disappeared around the side of the house. Christine heard the car door slam, and then the Camry backed out of the driveway.

Christine's mom shook her head sadly. "I'm sorry, Chrissie. I know this is a shock to you, but it has been really hard on him."

Christine stared out at the backyard, trying to digest what her parents had just told her. Then a wave of fear swept over her. "Do we have to sell the house? Do I still get to go to North Park?"

"We'll try to stay here. But don't say anything to your dad. He feels bad enough already."

"What does he do now? I mean, where is he going to work?" Christine's voice shook slightly.

"He's had a couple of interviews, but nothing has worked out yet. He's, well, he's older than some of the other candidates for these jobs. And it's a tough market right now."

"But there are lots of companies out there, right?"

Her mom nodded. "That's true. But your dad went on stress leave from Wood Grierson before they — I mean, before he left the company. So it's a little more complicated."

Christine wanted to ask what her mom meant by stress leave, and she wondered why her father decided to leave a perfectly good job. But something on her mother's face told her that now was not the time for more questions.

Over the last year or so, Christine had sensed that her father was bothered by something. He worked long hours and almost every weekend as a manager at a manufacturing plant. Sometimes days would pass without Christine seeing him. Her mother was in charge of several committees and spent many hours at the country club, where she played lots of tennis and golf.

Now Christine was starting to understand what had been bothering her dad. In a way, she was relieved. Her parents weren't splitting up, which had been her secret fear. Her dad had to find a new job — no big deal.

She went upstairs and was about to call Allie when she heard her parents talking downstairs.

"Did you tell her about the club?" she heard her father ask.

"Rob, I couldn't. It's too much for her to take in. We can tell her later," Monica replied.

Christine carefully opened her bedroom door so she could hear what her parents were saying.

"She has to learn that things have changed," Christine heard her father insist.

"But her friends all go to the club," Monica argued. "And she told Allie and Brittany that she would be going to the tennis camp. Couldn't they make an exception, even if we have cancelled the membership? We certainly gave them enough business over the time we've lived here."

"I'm not going to beg for charity," Rob answered sharply.

"All right, let me handle it. But Christine doesn't need to know," Monica insisted.

Christine sadly closed her door. Oh well, she thought, Dad will get a job soon and nobody at North Park High will ever have to know.

The next day, Christine called Allie and Brittany and the three girls met at Brittany's house. They sat by the pool, and Christine told them the news. The other girls were dumbfounded. Their parents had never lost a job. A couple of their classmates had dads who had been laid off. Those families had left abruptly and had never been heard from again. The only sign that they had ever been there was the real estate sign on the front lawns of their large houses and the empty desks in the classroom.

"At least your mom says that you're staying in Toronto," Allie said, trying to cheer her friend up.

"That means we'll all still go to North Park. That's what really counts, Chrissie," Brittany smiled. She got up and gave her friend a quick hug.

Christine smiled to herself. Brittany's reaction was so predictable; everything, in some way, revolved around her. But she was right. What really mattered was that they were still all together.

"Did you remember to sign up for tennis camp? It starts this afternoon," Brittany asked Allie, abruptly changing the subject.

Allie nodded. "My parents weren't too happy. They wanted me to help with a charity home-building project that they're part of. I had to agree to do that part of the day after tennis camp."

Brittany rolled her eyes and turned to Christine. "And you're signed up."

Christine felt her face flush with embarrassment as she remembered her parents' conversation. "Uh, I, uh ..."

"Oh, don't worry. It's all taken care of," Brittany waved her hand.

Christine gave her friend a puzzled look.

"You didn't tell me that your family had quit the club," Brittany said, giving her friend a stern look. "You should have told us."

Allie turned to Christine in surprise. Christine vehemently shook her head. "I didn't know," she replied tensely.

"Well, don't worry about it. I've called the club and made arrangements to put you under our membership. And you're signed up for the camp," Brittany explained coolly.

Christine was flustered. "I, uh, can't."

"It's all arranged. Don't worry about it," Brittany concluded.

Later that afternoon at the tennis camp, as she sat waiting for her turn to play, Christine fumed as she thought about the way Brittany had taken charge of the situation. She was angry that her friends had found out about her family's money troubles. And she was annoyed that Brittany thought she could just boss her around like that.

"I should have said no to Brittany paying for the camp," Christine muttered, as Allie sat down next to her, sweating from the exertion of her game.

"Why? She only wanted to help," Allie replied, taking a sip from her water bottle and offering some to Christine.

"Yeah, but she should have asked me, not told me," Christine persisted, frustrated that Allie was taking Brittany's side.

"She always gets her way. You should know that by now."

"And why is that?" Christine was starting to get really annoyed with her friend.

"Because she needs everyone to like her," Allie answered and pushed Christine up off the bench. "Your turn to play."

Christine glared over at Brittany, who was busy flirting with one of the instructors. She gave Christine a playful wave. Christine just looked away.

Chapter Two

MOVING

A few days later, Christine came home to find her dad out on the deck, sipping champagne.

"Hey, we've been waiting for you," her father said, enthusiastically. "We've got great news."

"Ta-da," her mother announced, walking out of the kitchen on to the deck. She was carrying a platter of lobsters. Christine gave her parents a puzzled look.

"We're celebrating," her father explained.

"Your father has a new job," his wife beamed. Monica put the platter down and gave Christine a hug.

"We're headed to Prince Edward Island," Rob exclaimed, punching his hand in the air. He grabbed a lobster and his wife, and danced a little jig around the deck. Rob took Christine by the arm and swung her around playfully. She stared at them blankly.

"Aren't you excited, Chrissie? This is a new start for all of us," her mom said cheerily.

"Great," Christine said, giving her mother and then father a lukewarm hug.

As her parents cracked their lobsters and munched away on the rich white meat dipped in butter, Christine sat silently, picking away at her lobster. Her dad explained that he had been asked to take over managing a big potato-processing plant on Prince Edward Island.

"It's a great opportunity." He beamed at his wife and daughter. "They're on the cutting edge of the industry with all the latest technology. And it's secure, too. The company has been around for a long time."

"Do you remember those *Anne of Green Gables* books, Christine?" Monica said.

"I don't think I ever read them, Mom," Christine mumbled, pushing aside her lobster. She watched as her father jokingly tossed his empty lobster claw into the shrubs. "A little souvenir for the next owners." He gave Christine an encouraging wink, but she just looked away.

"Honey, you'll have to read them before we go. PEI sounds like such a beautiful place in the books. I'm sure you're going to love it." Her mother smiled. Monica went on to describe the story of the orphan Anne who was adopted by a kindly old brother and sister and went to live in a place called Green Gables.

Christine hardly heard a word her mother said. She wasn't sure what to do. She wanted her father to be happy. But she didn't want to move. Tears welled up in her eyes.

After she loaded the dishwasher, Christine rushed to her room. She had to call Brittany and Allie and break the news to them. She called Brittany first.

"Prince Edward Island?" Brittany gasped, "Why would your dad take a job in Prince Edward Island?"

Allie was equally surprised when Christine called her. "What about North Park High? I mean, we've waited for years to go there. Together."

Christine struggled to keep from crying. "This is the meanest thing my parents have ever done to me," she exclaimed in a shaky voice. "I don't believe this is happening," she sobbed, finally letting the tears flow down her face.

The next afternoon, the three girls huddled together in Brittany's room, passing a box of Kleenex from one to the other.

"So, what are we going to do?" Christine finally managed to get the words out. Brittany had gone to the kitchen to get them some Diet Coke, microwave popcorn and a couple of cartons of chocolate-chocolate chip ice cream. The three girls now munched away quietly.

"What do you mean?" said Allie. "What is there to do?"

"I just thought you two might have some bright ideas," Christine said quietly. "Like, maybe, I could move in with you ..." She looked longingly around Brittany's room, which was more like an apartment than a bedroom. Brittany's parents were both real estate agents and were never home. She had been virtually raised by Francesca, the family housekeeper. Christine didn't think Brittany's parents would even notice she was there.

"I'd like to have you stay here, Chrissie, but you really have to go with your parents."

"But, for sure, you'll have to come back and visit us," Allie jumped in, giving her friend a hug. "You can stay at my house any time," she added.

"Well, why don't I just stay? With you," Christine suggested, brightening.

"C'mon, Chrissie. We don't have enough room at my house. Besides, you really do have to go with your mom and dad," Allie answered.

Christine was suddenly annoyed. "You keep saying that. Why do I have to go? Did they ask me? Did they even consider my feelings? No." Christine was too worn out to cry any more. She stared with red, glassy eyes at her best friends. They shrugged their shoulders. There wasn't much more to say.

The "For Sale" sign went up the next day. Christine felt as though all the neighbours were staring at her every time she rode her bicycle down the cul-de-sac.

Her parents didn't seem at all sad about saying goodbye to their old lives in Toronto. A moving van was booked, and the Millers began filling up boxes. Christine bumped into her dad, happily packing away his tools in the garage.

"You know what, Chrissie?" he said, pausing to blow the dust off one of his fancy saws. "I can't wait to take this stuff out again in Charlottetown and get back to working with my hands. I've really missed that."

When she was little, Christine spent hours in the garage watching her dad with his woodworking projects. He would ask her questions about her friends, about school and always, about her soccer team. That had stopped when he moved into management and started working long hours. But now Christine was too angry with her father to even admit how much she missed the time they used to spend together.

"I still can't believe you're doing this to me," she muttered, picking up one of the birdhouses they had built together years ago.

"There's no sense rehashing this," her father replied. He took the birdhouse gently from his daughter. "We'll have to find a special spot for this at the new house. We better look for a neighbourhood with trees this time."

"What do I hear about trees?" Monica came into the garage.

"A neighbourhood with trees this time?" Rob asked her, holding up the birdhouse. His wife gave him the thumbs up.

Christine scowled as she watched her parents cheerfully packing away their familiar lives in Toronto. She noticed that her parents were getting along better now that they were leaving Toronto. Christine had always thought her mom was pretty. Monica had curly brown hair, with only a few strands of gray, and Christine had inherited her brown eyes. Like her daughter, she was quite athletic and still played most sports competitively, even though she was now in her late forties. Christine's dad also looked quite young for his age. Today he was wearing his favourite worn Expos cap, hiding his thinning blonde hair. He was only slightly taller than his wife, and slim. He always teased Christine that his jeans were the same waist size as hers.

"If no one buys the house, do we get to stay?" Christine asked suddenly. Her parents stopped what they were doing and stared at her. They exchanged exasperated looks.

"It's time to let this go, Chrissie. We're going. It's final," Monica said.

"This is so unfair. You didn't ask me what I wanted. Did you?" The words and tears came tumbling out.

"There is nothing to ask. We're a family. Where your father goes, we go," her mother replied.

"And how is that fair?"

"Would you prefer that I sit here unemployed for the rest of my life?" Rob said in a quiet voice.

Christine grabbed the birdhouse from the box her father was packing but it slipped from her fingers and fell to the ground. The roof fell off and the walls collapsed. Christine gasped, then ran out of the garage. The last thing she saw was the hurt expression on her father's face as he stared at the broken birdhouse.

As the days went by, Christine kept hoping for a miracle — that her parents would change their minds, or announce that they were just joking and they weren't going to Prince Edward Island after all. All too soon, the moving van was packed. The family loaded their essential gear into the Jeep, in preparation for the drive to their new home.

It was their last night, and Brittany and Allie insisted on taking Christine out for dinner at Luigi's. Monica Miller dropped Allie and Christine off at the restaurant. Brittany was going to meet them there after her private tennis lesson.

"Have a super time, girls," Monica said cheerfully. Christine turned her back and walked towards the restaurant without a word.

"Thanks, Mrs. Miller. Have a great trip," Allie replied.

Christine fumed silently as the girls were shown to their table.

"It's not a trip, Allie. We're not coming back," Christine snapped at her friend. Allie looked hurt.

"Maybe this isn't such a good idea," Christine added, tensely tapping the menu on the table.

"Chrissie, can we just enjoy our last night together. Please." Allie's eyes pleaded with her friend.

Christine shrugged.

"I wish you were coming to North Park with us, Chrissie," Allie added quietly. "I'm not so sure that it's going to be as great as we think. The North Park kids at the club are such total snobs. I don't know. It's just not my kind of place. Brittany will be fine, but I'm not sure I'll fit in. It would have been a lot easier if you were there too."

Christine looked at her friend with surprise. Allie always appeared so confident on the surface, almost as self-assured as Brittany, although with Brittany a lot of the confidence was really an act. Christine knew that Allie sometimes tried too hard to fit in with whatever group she was hanging around with. But she had never suspected that her friend worried about high school. She wished there was something she could say.

"I wonder what PEI will be like," Allie continued. "You might really like it, Chrissie."

"Why would I like it? Everyone I know lives here," Christine replied, looking at her friend in disbelief.

"I'm sure there's life beyond Toronto. I still miss Peterborough sometimes," Allie answered. Christine gave her friend a surprised look.

"You were in kindergarten when you left there. How can you even remember?" she asked.

"We still go back to visit my grandma," Allie explained. "We all go hiking and camping and stuff like that."

"Gee, I somehow can't imagine Brittany hiking or camping," Christine giggled, and the two girls burst into laughter.

Just then, Brittany arrived, waving a beautifully wrapped box.

"Open it, open it!" Brittany insisted as she sat down at the table.

Christine tore open the package. Inside was a cellular phone. Christine gasped.

"This is your direct line to us, any time day or night," Brittany said.

Later, as they spooned up the last of their spumoni ice cream, Christine looked over at Allie and thought back to her friend's comments earlier that evening about not really liking Toronto. She wondered if Allie was just trying to make her feel better. She couldn't believe that anyone would actually prefer PEI to North Park High.

Brittany raised her water glass in Christine's direction and made a toast.

"We are all going to have a great Grade Nine," Brittany announced. "Even you, Christine."

Chapter Three

THE ISLAND

*C*hristine took a deep breath as her family's Jeep started up the ramp to the Confederation Bridge, crossing from the mainland on to Prince Edward Island. She was about to leave her old life behind and start a new one. As they arrived on the small island province, Christine scanned the rolling farm fields.

"This is truly boring," she said. "What is there to do here?"

Monica Miller looked at her daughter in the back seat and gave her an encouraging smile. "I think it's wonderful," she replied, gesturing enthusiastically at the passing scenery. Black and white cows munched grass peacefully on a rolling green hillside. On the other side of the highway, field after field of potato plants waved lazily in the warm breeze. "It's so peaceful and picturesque."

"They're good people here, too," Christine's dad added. He hummed away, tapping the steering wheel in time to the music on the radio. Christine pulled on the head set of her Walkman and turned up the volume, slouching down in the backseat.

As they approached Charlottetown, Christine checked the horizon for the familiar office towers and high-rise apartment buildings of Toronto. But as they drove through the capital city, all she saw were tree-lined residential streets, with the occasional church or school scattered along the route.

Her dad finally found the hotel where they were staying the night. Christine was tempted to stay in the car and demand that they head back to Ontario, but she sensed that her parents were in no mood to hear any more of her complaints.

The next day Christine's mom drove her to Queen Charlotte Intermediate School, a ten-minute drive from their hotel.

"See how close everything is here," Monica said enthusiastically, sensing her daughter's low spirits. "No more traffic jams, no more commutes. It's going to be wonderful."

Christine just stared out the window.

The streets of Charlottetown were much narrower than the ones in Toronto. There were no skyscrapers, no subway stops and not a lot of traffic. The streets were lined with trees and modest houses. On the main drag along University Avenue, Christine spotted the familiar signs of McDonald's and KFC. Well, at least, there's fast food here, she thought sourly to herself.

They arrived in front of Queen Charlotte, a modern two-story building in the midst of a nice neighbourhood. Teenagers were already streaming into the front doors. Christine stared at them for any sign of familiar fashions. To her surprise, the girls were wearing many of the same styles as her friends back home in Toronto. Most had on jeans and tee-shirts, with all the familiar brand names. Many of the guys wore track suits, sneakers and baseball caps. Almost everyone carried a knapsack.

"It looks like a nice enough school," Christine's mom said. "Let's go in and meet everyone, honey," her mother said, sympathetically, touching Christine gently on the arm.

Christine bristled. This move was her mother's fault as much as her father's. She grabbed the door handle, angrily throwing the car door open. She stormed off towards the building.

She noticed some of the younger students heading towards the side door. Christine rolled her eyes. Grade Sevens, she sneered to herself. She couldn't believe she was going to be stuck at a school with Grade-Seven and -Eight kids again. At home she and her friends had counted the days until they were finally moving on to high school. Not anymore, Christine thought sourly to herself. She noticed that the older kids gathered in groups around the main door. They all stared at Christine and her mother as they walked past, not even bothering to avert their curious looks. "How rude," Christine muttered under her breath. Her mother gave her a stern look.

Just inside the door, Christine and her mom were met by a girl with short, reddish hair. She was wearing jeans and a Nike tee-shirt, and she waved cheerfully in their direction.

"Hi, you must be Christine Miller," the girl said, picking up a knapsack off the floor. "I'm Jennifer Gallant."

"How do you know who I am?" Christine asked.

"Well, almost everyone here has grown up together so I know pretty well everyone in the school. You were the first person to walk through the doors I didn't know." Jennifer grinned. She led the Millers across the hallway to the principal's office.

Christine sighed to herself. Everyone knew everyone else here. She would be the outsider and a reluctant one at that. She could only imagine what they would think of someone moving here from Toronto. A loser, she thought to herself, because that's what I am.

As they walked down the hallway, Christine took a furtive look over at Jennifer. She had freckles and friendly green eyes.

Christine noticed Jennifer's running shoes and decided that she must be interested in sports. There was something very athletic about the Island girl that reminded Christine of herself. Still, she was determined not to like anything or anyone in her new school.

Christine stood silently as her mother chatted away with Mr. Carruthers, the principal.

"We're so thrilled to be here," Monica explained. "We just love what we've seen of the Island so far."

"And will you be joining any of our sports teams — or maybe the drama club or newspaper?" Mr. Carruthers asked Christine kindly.

"I don't think so," Christine said quietly, eyes on the floor.

Her mother looked annoyed. "Christine has played soccer for years. And she is a very good runner."

"I'll be sure to mention that to our soccer coach," Mr. Carruthers replied.

Christine stood there, mute. Don't bother, she thought to herself.

The first day of school was a blur to Christine. Jennifer stuck with her most of the day, pretending not to notice that Christine said hardly one word to her and made no effort to talk to anyone else at the school. When the final bell sounded, Christine rushed off without saying goodbye or thank you to Jennifer. As Christine turned the corner, she paused and could hear Jennifer and her friends talking about her.

"What a snob," said Melanie, one of Jennifer's classmates.

"I guess she thinks she's hot stuff because she's from Toronto," added Ashley, as the girls grabbed their gym clothes from their lockers so they could get changed for volleyball practice.

"Another CFA Just what we need," Melanie replied. Christine cringed. Her dad had told her that Islanders referred to newcomers as CFAs — meaning Come From Aways. If you weren't born on the Island, you were a CFA, no matter how long you lived there.

"Yep, those Upper Canadians think they own the country," Jennifer said and the girls all laughed. Christine was about to leave when she heard Jennifer again. "I don't think she's a snob, Mel. I don't think she wanted to move here. How would you like it?"

Christine turned away sadly and headed towards the door.

"How did it go?" Monica asked, as she picked up Christine outside Queen Charlotte. They headed downtown to meet a real estate agent to look at some houses.

"I don't want to talk about it," said Christine. "Can you just drop me back at the hotel?"

"Don't you want to see the houses that we're looking at?" her mother urged.

"I don't care," Christine muttered.

Her mother reluctantly dropped Christine off at the hotel. As soon as she got to the room, Christine pulled out the cellular phone her friends had given her. She quickly dialled Brittany's number. It was busy. She tried Allie's house. Her line was busy too.

"They must be talking to each other." Christine smiled, imagining the two of them going over the day's events, dissecting every person's wardrobe and who was talking to whom in the hallways.

But Christine's smile soon turned to a frown as she kept trying her friends' numbers and couldn't get through. She knew her parents would be back in about an hour and she desperately needed to talk to Brittany and Allie. They should have known that Christine would be calling to get all the news.

"We should have set up a time for me to call," Christine muttered, getting another busy signal. Finally, frustrated, she threw the cell phone against the pillow and fell on the bed, in tears.

After several minutes of sobbing, Christine grabbed her jean jacket and raced out of the hotel. Her eyes still blinded with tears, she headed towards the waterfront. Eventually she stopped crying and started looking around. She climbed a steep hill where a line of cannons overlooked the water and dropped down onto the grass.

I can't stay here, Christine thought to herself, staring out across the water. Toronto is where I belong, not this place, she told herself. She examined the unfamiliar horizon, hugging her knees to her chest and rocking back and forth. A few walkers strolled by but no one paid any attention to her.

As the minutes passed, the sun hid behind the clouds and late-day shadows formed across the boardwalk. Christine looked at her watch. She had been gone for more than an hour. She suddenly realized that she hadn't even left a note for her parents. They were sure to worry when they got back and discovered she wasn't at the hotel.

"Too bad," she muttered angrily, stretching her stiff legs and shivering slightly as the sun started to drop towards the horizon. The skyline was vast and beautiful, with the red cliffs across the water from Charlottetown glowing with the setting sun.

Gazing out over the water again, Christine noticed a light in the distance she hadn't seen before. She squinted and looked again. There, on the tip of land just before the harbour opened up into the Northumberland Strait, was a red and white lighthouse. Christine stared in fascination as pulses of bright, white light danced across the waves of the harbour. The powerful beacon was like a messenger from far away, telling her, gently, soothingly, that everything would work out.

Suddenly, she knew what she had to do. She would go back to Toronto on her own. Her friends would change their minds and let her stay with them once they saw she was serious. Christine felt revitalized. She raced along the boardwalk, her head full of plans for her trip back to Ontario.

When she opened the door to their hotel room, her mother came rushing to greet her. "Oh, thank goodness you're all right," Monica gasped, giving Christine a hug.

"Where have you been, young lady?" her father growled.

His wife glared at him. "We were worried, Chrissie," she said gently. "This is a new city and we had no idea where you had gone. You could have left us a note."

Christine was about to apologize when her father dangled the cellular phone in front of her. "And what is this?" he asked.

"It's a cell phone," Christine answered.

"Yes, I realize that. Whose cell phone?" her father continued.

"Mine."

"Since when?"

"It was my going-away present," Christine explained. "From Brittany and Allie."

"And who is going to pay the monthly charges?" he inquired.

"They are," Christine murmured.

"I don't think so," her father answered. "We may not be in the same income bracket as the Walkers and the O'Donnells, but you are certainly not going to be financially dependent on those girls. You're sending it back." He put the cell phone away in a corner of his suitcase and left the room without another word. Christine sank onto the bed, shaking her head in disbelief.

"What's his problem?" she asked her mother, who stared after her husband.

"He thinks you're still mad at him for bringing us here," Monica replied.

"I am mad," Christine answered. "In fact, this totally sucks. I don't want to be here. Let's go home."

"It's not that easy." Her mother sighed. "Your father couldn't find a good job in Toronto. It took months to find the job here. And he felt that everyone in our neighbourhood was looking down on him because he was out of work."

Christine didn't know what to say. "That's stupid. Who cares what anyone else thinks?"

Monica shrugged. "I think it was time for a change, for all of us. I like it better here already. You should have seen some of the houses we looked at today. The one we liked the best is really old, a big Victorian place and beautifully renovated. You'll love it."

Christine didn't have the heart to tell her mother that she had no intention of staying. She'd break the news once her plans were in place. For now, she needed to keep her mother on her side.

"Can we go have supper now?" she suggested.

"Sure thing." Her mother smiled. "I just need a minute to freshen up."

Chapter Four

PHONE HOME

As soon as her mother left the room, Christine rummaged through her dad's suitcase. She found the cell phone and hid it in the pocket of her jean jacket. She had to talk to Brittany and Allie as soon as possible if she was going to make her plan work.

The Millers walked across the street to a tiny Italian restaurant. Sirenella's was filled with photographs of Italy and the familiar smell of garlic, and the owner greeted them warmly at the door.

Christine played with her fettucine at supper as her parents talked enthusiastically about the new house. Watching them, part of her wished she could share in their excitement but her mind was made up. After they ate, Christine excused herself to go to the washroom. Pulling out the cell phone, she quickly dialled Brittany's number. To her relief, the call went through right away.

"Oh Britt, thank goodness you finally answered," Christine gasped, hiding in the bathroom stall, praying her mother wouldn't come looking for her just yet.

"Chrissie, what's up?" Brittany sounded slightly surprised. Christine wondered why. After all, they used to talk to each other every day.

"This is a nightmare," Christine began. "I hate it here and my dad took the cell phone away and ..."

Suddenly Brittany interrupted. "I've got another call, Chrissie. Hang tight for just a minute," Brittany said, then disappeared off the line.

Christine was startled. She couldn't believe that her friend was taking another call in the middle of her crisis. What could possibly be more important?

The minutes ticked by. Fortunately no one else had come in to the washroom yet, but Christine knew her parents would soon be suspicious. Where was Brittany?

After what seemed like hours, Brittany re-appeared on the line.

"Sorry, Chrissie, but I've got to go. Martin Drake is on the other line. Can you believe it?" she squealed. "I was so excited I forgot that you were on hold," Brittany added with a giggle. "I'll call you back, Chrissie."

"No, you can't do that!" Christine snapped. She couldn't believe her friend was acting like such an idiot.

"Okay, okay, calm down," Brittany replied.

"You don't understand," Christine sobbed.

"Christine, not now," Brittany pleaded. "I'll call you tomorrow. Just keep the cell phone on. Talk to ya."

"Call me at lunch," Christine blurted out, but her friend had already hung up. Christine quickly hid the phone in her pocket. She hurried back to the table, where her parents were still deep in conversation. She noticed that her mother was beaming as they talked about the new house. They hardly noticed when Christine returned.

"And, Chrissie, I've already picked out a spot for the birdhouse," Rob said, grinning. Christine shrugged and focused her attention on her cheesecake, hoping her father would change the subject. Rob paused for a moment, as if he was hoping she would say something else. Then he turned back to Monica.

"Do you want to dig a perennial bed this fall or should we wait until spring?" he pondered.

As her parents talked about their new garden, Christine replayed the conversation with Brittany over and over in her mind. She couldn't believe how rude her friend had been, especially considering how upset Christine was. And what was the big deal about Martin Drake? She vaguely recognized the name. He was some hotshot guy in Grade Eleven that the girls had seen a couple of times at the country club. Christine felt a surge of jealousy. After all, if she had been at North Park High, she might have been the one on the phone with Martin.

Christine had always known that Brittany was full of herself, but this afternoon had proved it. She wished she had called Allie first. Allie had her head screwed on straight. She would be able to come up with a plan to help Christine.

Christine smiled as she thought about what a good friend Allie was, and she wished she could get in touch with her right now. The cell phone lay hidden under her jacket. It was turned off now. Christine couldn't risk the phone ringing with her parents close by. All she could do was hope that her friends called her back tomorrow.

The next day, Christine put the phone in her knapsack. She asked her mother to drop her off early at Queen Charlotte. "I have to meet some of the girls in my class to go over an assignment," Christine lied.

Monica gave Christine an encouraging smile as she got out of the car. "Good luck with your project," she called.

Christine felt a few twinges of guilt at her mother's cheery goodbye. As soon as her mother was out of sight, Christine sat on the school steps, pulled out the cell phone and turned it on.

She waited for it to ring, but it remained silent. She didn't dare phone Allie in case her line was busy when Brittany called. Finally, Christine threw the phone into her knapsack in frustration and ran to class.

At lunchtime, Christine hurried to the parking lot and pulled the phone again. Still it didn't ring. Where were Brittany and Allie? she wondered. She wanted to call, but looking at her watch, she realized that with the time difference, her friends would be in class right now.

Christine spent the lunch hour pacing the parking lot, formulating her plan to run away. She would have to borrow some money from Brittany or Allie for the plane ticket home. She could fly student stand-by, so it wouldn't be too expensive. She could get lots of work babysitting on weekends, and she was sure that her parents would eventually relent and help support her, once they realized that she was intent on staying in Toronto.

Later that afternoon Christine sat staring into space in English class as Ms. Franklin talked about the origins of the Shakespearean sonnet. Jennifer Gallant had saved her a seat at the front of the class but Christine walked right by, mumbling something about being far-sighted. She knew it was a lame excuse but she just wasn't in the mood to be friendly right now.

Just as Ms. Franklin was in the middle of reading the first sonnet, there was a ringing sound from Christine's knapsack. Horrified, Christine realized it was the cell phone. She froze for a moment, not sure what to do.

"Well, you might as well answer it," Ms. Franklin said sharply, as the entire class turned to look at Christine.

She scrambled through the knapsack but by the time she grabbed the phone, it had stopped ringing. She turned the phone off and dropped it back into her knapsack. There was a wave of whispers through the room, and everyone continued to stare, including the teacher.

Christine had enough. "What?" she sneered, "Have you never seen a cellular phone before?"

That provoked even more laughter from the class. Ms. Franklin tossed her book down on the desk and motioned to Christine to come up to the front.

"And bring your little cellular phone with you," she added. "I don't know what kind of school you're used to wherever you're from, but here we apologize when we cause a disruption in class," the teacher said pointedly.

Ms. Franklin was thirty-something, one of the younger teachers at the school. Today, she was wearing a black turtleneck and black jeans, with a nice pair of cowboy boots. Under other circumstances, Christine probably would have thought she was pretty cool. But as things stood right now, she didn't. And she was shocked that the teacher was making such a big deal over a cell phone. She wondered why Ms. Franklin was picking on her.

"Oh, I'm sorry all right," Christine muttered. "I missed my call."

As soon as the words were out, Christine realized she had made a big mistake. A look of fury passed over Ms. Franklin's face and she motioned for Christine to follow her out to the hallway.

"Come with me," she snapped.

When they reached the principal's office, Christine waited outside as the teacher explained what had happened. She caught the odd fragment of what Ms. Franklin was saying. Christine heard "Spoiled brat," "Too good for us," "Back to Toronto" and "Call her parents."

About fifteen minutes later, a pale-faced Monica Miller appeared at the office. She was escorted in to see the principal, then Christine was finally called in.

"I'm sorry these are the circumstances under which we meet again," Mr. Carruthers began. He was a distinguished-looking man, tall and graying, with a booming voice.

"I would like you to apologize, first of all, to Ms. Franklin," he continued. "No one needs to be treated this way, particularly a teacher that you have just met," Mr. Carruthers added and then paused.

"I'm sorry," Christine mumbled, not able to meet her mother's gaze.

"Furthermore, your cellular phone will not be allowed on the premises," Mr. Carruthers continued.

"I understand," Christine replied in a subdued voice.

"Let's put this behind us and get off to a fresh start tomorrow," Mr. Carruthers concluded. He shook hands with Christine's mom and then escorted them to the door. Just then the bell rang and the students rushed by to make the school bus. Christine noticed that several pointed at her and snickered as they pushed through the hallway.

When they got to the Jeep, Monica sighed. "I thought we were going to try to make this work, Christine."

"I want to go home," Christine answered, staring out the window. "I was calling Brittany and Allie to borrow some money. I'm going back to Toronto."

Monica clutched the steering wheel and said nothing for a moment. "We have to talk about this, Christine," she said finally, her voice filled with disappointment.

Back at the hotel, Christine's dad fumed silently as Monica told him about the phone incident. Christine sat sullenly as her mother described her embarrassment. He rolled his eyes when his wife told him about Christine's plan to return to Toronto.

"This will go no further," Rob said. He put the cell phone into his pocket. "As for going back to Toronto, that will not happen. I've had enough of your whining. We're here. Get used to it. You are also grounded for the next week. Not that it will make any difference as you obviously have decided to alienate every single person that you meet here. Am I clear?"

Christine nodded, knowing better than to argue. Later that night, after her parents went to bed, she heard them whispering in the other room.

"I know I was too hard on her today," Rob said quietly. "But she has to let go."

"Yelling at her won't make her forget her friends any faster," Monica replied. "It takes time. Let's just give her time."

Christine sighed. Her mother was wrong this time. Only a trip back home would make things right. She needed to get back to Toronto, and fast.

Chapter Five

THE PROJECT BEGINS

*T*he next few days were a blur of unpacking boxes as the Millers moved into their new home in Brighton, a neighbourhood in downtown Charlottetown. The area was filled with stately, old houses, very different from the modern neighbourhood where the family had lived in Toronto. There, their house had been carpeted, with white walls and all the modern conveniences. Their new home was very old, with hardwood floors and creaky stairs.

"Where are the closets?" Christine gasped, when her mother showed her to her room.

"I'm afraid they weren't into big closets when this house was built." Her mother chuckled. "A girl of your age in the Victorian era would only have had a few dresses and she would have kept them in a wardrobe."

"I guess we kind of forget how different things were for kids back then," Christine replied, looking at the piles of clothes and shoes and CDs littering the floor.

Monica went from room to room directing the movers. She had already arranged to have the master bedroom painted a rich green colour — very different from the bland, beige walls of their house in Toronto.

"I've been watching the newspaper for some auctions," Monica explained. "I'm going to stock this place with antiques. I hear you can get some great deals."

Christine was surprised to see this side of her mother's personality. Monica often talked nostalgically about her childhood in Pembroke, a small town on the Ottawa River, but Christine had always assumed that her mom was happy in Toronto with charity work and social activities. She had given up her job as a librarian at York University when Christine was born. Since they had moved to Charlottetown though, her mom seemed intent on expanding her horizons. She was talking about taking a few university courses and maybe even getting a part-time job.

"I've always wanted to live in a house like this. It has so much more character and history," Monica explained to Christine as they unpacked some of their dishes and stacked them in the kitchen cupboards.

"I thought you liked the house in Toronto," Christine said.

"Oh, it was all right, I guess," Monica sighed. "But, you know, coming from a small town, I always found Toronto a little impersonal. I missed having neighbours I could talk to. I never really felt I belonged with the country club crowd."

"Does that mean we'll never go back to Toronto?"

"I don't know, Chrissie. Does it really mean that much to you?"

"Yes, I think it does,"Christine replied seriously.

Monica sighed. "I know this doesn't help much now, but I promise you it will get better."

That was not much consolation to Christine. She hid her face in a cupboard so her mother wouldn't see her teary eyes.

After a busy weekend of settling into the new house, Christine was sorry to return to school on Monday. She found herself sitting next to Jennifer Gallant again in Social Studies class. Jennifer gave Christine a shy smile as she settled into her seat.

"How did the unpacking go?" she asked Christine.

"Okay," Christine muttered, keeping her eyes on her notebook.

"Brighton's a nice area," Jennifer continued, trying to keep the conversation going.

"It's okay, I guess," Christine replied.

"It's kind of old, though," Christine added.

"Oh, I know. I love those historic houses," Jennifer said. "And you're nice and close to the boardwalk."

"Yeah, I like it down there," Christine admitted grudgingly.

Just then, the teacher called the class to order. Jennifer looked disappointed.

"Maybe we can go down to the boardwalk later?" she whispered. Christine pretended she couldn't hear her and turned her attention to the teacher.

"I'd like you to work in groups of two and prepare a presentation about an issue in the news," Ms. Carpenter, their Social Studies teacher, explained. "It can be a national or international issue, or even something local."

"Do you want to work together?" Jennifer asked.

Christine nodded reluctantly.

"Why don't you come to my house after school and we can get started on our project?" Jennifer asked.

The girls met at the front doors after school. Jennifer lived downtown, within walking distance of Christine's house. They stopped by the Millers' place on the way.

"Nice to see you again," Christine's mom smiled, obviously pleased to see her daughter making an effort to fit in.

"We're just heading over to Jennifer's to work on a project for Social Studies class," Christine explained, her eyes pleading with her mother to allow her to go. She didn't want to mention that she was supposed to be grounded in front of Jennifer.

"What's your project about?" Monica asked, nodding her approval.

"We don't know yet. We're going to do some research at my house," Jennifer explained.

"Well, good luck," Monica yelled after them as they headed out the door.

"Your mom is really pretty," Jennifer said. "How's she liking it here?"

"Oh, she loves it, especially all the history and the ocean, of course," Christine replied.

"And your dad?"

"He's pretty busy learning the ropes at his new company but he's sure not as stressed as he was in Toronto."

"So you're the only one who doesn't like it here," Jennifer said in a matter-of-fact voice.

Christine was startled by the other girl's honesty. "It's that obvious?"

"I guess so," Jennifer replied. "I mean, I understand. You come from a big city where there's lots of stuff to do. And I bet you have some great shopping there."

Christine laughed. "You mean you don't have the Gap here?"

"The what?" Jennifer said, teasingly. She was wearing a Gap tee-shirt and she flipped the label out of the back, pretending to try to read it.

Both the girls giggled. They walked down Great George Street to Jennifer's house, half a block from the harbour. Her father ran a fish store, and the family lived in an apartment above. They popped in the store to meet Jennifer's father.

"Pleasure to meet you," Patrick Gallant said. He was a burly man with graying hair and twinkling eyes.

"Nice to meet you," Christine said after a momentary pause. She was so busy looking around the shop that she almost forgot her manners. The front room was filled with artifacts from the sea — from pieces of driftwood and lobster traps hanging from the ceiling to giant painted buoys dangling from the walls. There were photographs everywhere. Christine was drawn instantly to a giant black and white photo of a lighthouse.

"She's a beauty, isn't she?" Patrick said, noticing Christine's interest.

"That's the Governors Lighthouse, out near the mouth of the harbour. You can see that one from the boardwalk," he explained.

"Yes, I've seen it," Christine said, with wonder in her voice. "I didn't realize it was so big."

"It looks tiny from shore, doesn't it?" Jennifer agreed.

"It's too bad they're talking now about tearing her down," Patrick grumbled. "Call it progress, they do. I call it a sin."

"Why are they going to tear it down?" Christine asked, surprised to find herself genuinely concerned.

"They don't actually tend the light anymore," Patrick explained. "It's all automated. And the ships that come into the harbour use radar to guide them. The government wants to get rid of all the old buildings."

"The local historical society is trying to save it, though, aren't they, Dad?" Jennifer asked.

"Aye," he answered. "But they've got a tough road ahead." He paused for a moment, lost in thought. "And that's not even the saddest part of all."

"What do you mean?" Christine asked, wide-eyed.

"There's an old couple living there. He used to be the lightkeeper. The government let him stay on when they went automated. But now they'll be losin' their home for sure." Patrick sighed, staring lovingly at the photo on the wall.

"That's terrible," Christine said, suddenly animated.

"I have an idea," Jennifer answered, a smile growing on her face. "Why don't we do our project about what's going to happen to the lighthouse?"

Christine wanted to share the Island girl's enthusiasm, but she had some misgivings about what she would be getting herself into. She liked the idea of doing a project about the lighthouse but she also knew that she probably wasn't going to be here to finish it. What should she do?

"Why not?" Christine said finally.

"Good luck to you girls," Patrick said, getting back to the counter to serve a customer.

As they went upstairs to the family's living quarters, Christine looked around curiously. She wondered what it would be like to have the noise and the smell of a store down below. The Gallants' part of the building was much bigger than it looked from outside. There was a living room, filled with antiques, including an old cast iron stove. Shelves on the walls were covered in brass bells and candlesticks. Christine didn't know a lot about antiques but she knew her mom would love the Gallants' place. It wasn't what Christine was used to. Brittany's house in Toronto had been filled with fancy modern art and leather furniture, and always looked impeccable, like something out of a magazine. The Gallants' home could have been in a magazine too, with all its antiques and fireplaces, but there was a cluttered, lived-in look that Christine liked.

Christine tried to concentrate as the girls went through back issues of the newspaper, looking for stories about the lighthouse. She wondered if Jennifer had noticed Christine's hesitation when she had suggested the lighthouse project.

"Here it is," Jennifer said, waving a copy of *The Guardian*. "'HERITAGE GROUP PROTESTS PLANNED DEMOLITION OF LIGHTHOUSE.' Do you want to take this and read it tonight?"

"Sure, my dad has a photocopier at home. I'll bring it in to class tomorrow," Christine promised.

As she made her way home through the streets of Charlottetown, Christine tried to sort out her confused emotions. She had enjoyed talking to Jennifer and meeting her father. She liked Jennifer, and if circumstances had been different, they might have become friends. But Christine had to get back to Toronto and so there was no sense making any friends here.

As she thought about Toronto, Christine felt pangs of homesickness. Just then she noticed a phone booth on the other side of the street. She rushed across and dialled the operator.

"Collect call please, from Christine Miller," she said breathlessly. Her heart skipped a beat as Allie answered and quickly accepted the charges.

"What's going on, Christine?" Allie asked sympathetically. "Brittany told me that you called. We tried to call you back the next day, but you never answered."

"Oh, Allie, it's a long story,"Christine sighed. "My dad got mad about the cell phone and took it away from me because I told him I was moving back to Toronto."

"You're doing what?" Allie sounded surprised. "How come?"

"I don't belong here. Everyone is nice enough but they've lived here all their lives. I belong at North Park High with you and Brittany." Christine continued breathlessly, not giving her friend time to interrupt. "I've got some money saved up from my allowance. I can work every weekend babysitting. Maybe my parents will even kick in some money once they get used to the idea. But I need some cash to get a plane ticket home. And a place to stay."

"Chrissie, I understand, really I do," Allie said, after a long pause. "But you can't just leave your family."

"We should never have moved here in the first place," Christine replied, frustration in her voice. "And I'm almost fourteen. It's time for me to start doing what's best for me, you know, in the long run."

"I don't know, Chrissie …"

"I don't want to stay with my parents. Not here." Christine's voice was starting to shake.

"I know you're mad at them," Allie replied, "but there's not much you can do. By the way, did you hear what Brittany has done? She's going out with Martin Drake. What am I supposed to do now?"

"I could care less right now, Allie," Christine snapped. "I've got big problems to deal with."

"Christine, I understand how you're feeling but yelling at me is not going to help. I have problems too," Allie said, a slight chill in her voice.

"Wait … I'm sorry. You've got to help me," Christine begged.

"I've got to meet Brittany in a few minutes. She has finally torn herself away from Martin long enough to call me," Allie answered. "If we can think of anything we can do, we'll call you. Okay? I don't know what else to say, Chrissie."

Christine stood silently, staring at the receiver, then slammed down the phone. She couldn't believe it. Her best friends in the world had given her the brush-off, just because she had moved to another city. They weren't going to call her back. She could hear the distance in Allie's tone. Their friendship was over. Christine started to cry as she headed along the waterfront towards her family's new home.

In the distance, Christine noticed the flickering glow of the Governors Lighthouse. She closed her eyes and tried to remember the familiar lights on the street in Toronto. But all she could see was the pulsing white flash of the lighthouse. When she opened her eyes, it was again just a flicker on the horizon.

"What are you trying to tell me?" she whispered. She shuddered suddenly, as a burst of wind bounced up along the rocky shore to where she stood. Pulling her jacket tighter, Christine reluctantly turned her back on the light and headed home into the dusky night.

Chapter Six

THE HISTORY
OF THE LIGHT

*T*he next day, Christine was still upset over the fight with her friends. She felt as if they had deserted her. She studied the faces in the hallway at Queen Charlotte anxiously, looking for anyone she recognized. She felt very alone. In Social Studies class, she made sure that she found a seat near Jennifer. Ms. Carpenter started to talk about the projects.

"I'll give you some class time today and on Friday to work on them. I'm going to go around the classroom now and find out what each group is planning," she directed the students, who broke into pairs and started to talk.

"What are the two of you up to?" Ms. Carpenter smiled as she perched on Jennifer's desk.

Jennifer pointed to the article in *The Guardian*. "We're going to look into the proposed demolition of the Governors Lighthouse and the old couple who live there."

"They've lived there for ages and now the government is

going to make them leave," Christine added.

Ms. Carpenter looked impressed. "That's a great idea. Have you talked to the McIntoshes yet?"

The girls shook their heads.

"I can give you the phone number for the president of the historical society," the teacher offered.

"Thanks," Jennifer said.

"Good luck," Ms. Carpenter added, before moving on to the next group.

"We need to get out to the lighthouse," Jennifer proposed.

"I'm sure my mother would take us," Christine suggested. "She loves old, historical stuff. This should be right up her alley."

That night at the supper table, Christine told her parents about the dispute over the Governors Lighthouse and the problems the McIntoshes were having.

"I'm going to call the McIntoshes after supper. I got their number from the historical society," she said. "If they agree to let us come out there, can you drive us, Mom? I mean, unless I'm still grounded."

"I think we can make an exception for this. And yes, I'd love to take you out there." Monica smiled as her daughter got up from the table and went out to the kitchen to make her phone call.

Christine hung around the door, just out of sight, as she heard her parents talking about her.

"She seems to be settling in, finally," Christine's dad said, pleased.

"Taking away the cellular phone was probably a little extreme but it seems to have worked," his wife replied.

"I'm glad to get her away from there," he continued. "We could never have afforded the kind of life that she and her friends wanted. That whole neighbourhood was one big snob factory. Christine would have become like all the rest of them."

"Rob, I think you've got to let it go now," Monica urged. "We're lucky that we have a chance for a fresh start here."

"We got Christine out of there just in the nick of time," he added, with a bitter tone to his voice.

"The people are nicer here," Monica admitted. "But I don't think you're giving Christine enough credit. I think she'd have been fine. It was her friends I worried about. I never liked those girls much. I always thought they were going to let her down someday."

Listening to her parents in the kitchen, Christine sighed. As much as she hated to admit it, her parents were right about Brittany and Allie.

She went upstairs to her room. It still felt unfamiliar, even with all her posters and books unpacked and organized the way they were back in Toronto. She closed her eyes and tried to imagine she was still there. She felt a wave of loneliness but shook it off as she dialled the number in the phone book for Betty and Dave McIntosh. A man answered on the first ring.

"Mr. McIntosh? My name is Christine Miller and my friend and I are doing a school project about the Governors Lighthouse," Christine explained. "We were wondering if it would be possible to come out and see the lighthouse in person."

"Well, my wife is very upset about all that's been going on," he replied. He had a thick Island accent and Christine strained to understand him.

"I think it's terrible what they're doing to you," Christine agreed. "I just moved here from Toronto. I can't imagine what it would be like to be kicked out of a home where you've lived for so many years."

"Yes, that's the long and the short of it," the old man answered. "Let me ask my wife what she thinks."

Christine waited on the line as he talked to his wife. If they didn't agree, the girls might have to find another project to do.

Mr. McIntosh picked up the phone. "When would you like to come?" he said.

"Can we come tomorrow after school?"

"See you then," Mr. McIntosh said kindly.

The next day at lunch, Christine sat with Jennifer and a group of her friends and they talked about what they wanted to ask the old couple. Christine left early to go to the library to do some more research before the afternoon classes began. She couldn't believe that she was going to get to see the lighthouse up close.

"Little Miss Toronto seems to be mellowing out," Christine heard Ashley say to Jennifer after Christine left their table. She hovered in the doorway, curious to hear what the girls had to say.

"She's not a snob, really," Jennifer replied.

"I don't trust these people from Toronto," Melanie observed.

Jennifer laughed and shook her head. "I think she's nice and she's getting right involved in this project about the lighthouse," she added.

"We'll see," Melanie insisted. They looked over in Christine's direction and she rushed out of the door, hoping they hadn't seen her. As she walked to the library, her mind was abuzz with what the girls had said. She wasn't a snob, she thought angrily. Brittany was a snob, and Allie too, she added sourly. Christine felt another wave of self-pity coming over her as she walked through the unfamiliar hallways of her new school. She had trouble finding the library but was too stubborn to ask for help. She felt as though everyone was looking at her.

When she got to the library, she summoned up her courage to ask the librarian for help.

"I'm looking for books about lighthouses," she said, her voice shaking slightly. Mrs. McCardle, the librarian, gestured for Christine to follow her. She showed Christine how to use the computer to check the library catalogue.

"We also have several computers with access to the Internet, if that would help with your search," she added. "Are you familiar with the Internet?"

"Uh-yeah," Christine stammered. She realized that she had assumed that they wouldn't even have Internet access at Queen Charlotte. Maybe I am a snob, she thought wryly.

She found a couple of books and a few articles that Mrs. McCardle photocopied for her out of the magazine of the Island historical society. By the time she finished signing out of the books, the bell rang for the afternoon classes.

That afternoon seemed to drag for Christine. She kept sneaking looks at the articles she had found in the school library. There was an entire book about the lighthouses of Atlantic Canada and she flipped eagerly to the section about the Governors Lighthouse.

The Islander reported the opening of the lighthouse in 1845. On Monday last, a committee appointed by the House of Assembly ... proceeded in ten sleighs across the harbour for the purpose of selecting a site for the intended Lighthouse. The land was surveyed by Mr. Gall and the clearing of the woods for the building disposed of to persons from the neighboring settlement. The party partook of a lunch and returned across the harbour.

Christine caught her breath as she imagined the old-fashioned sleighs racing across the harbour with "British colours gaily flying." She wondered what it would have been like, huddled under fur blankets, clutching hot-water pans to stay warm, with the crisp cold wind blowing directly into the faces of the horses and travellers as they crossed the ice.

She read on. Originally, the lightkeepers used primitive oil lamps, which were incredibly time-consuming to maintain. Cleaning them was a daily chore for the lightkeepers who often lived in adjoining buildings and worked long hours. In the late 1800s, the lamps were replaced by ground glass lenses that reflected the light beams out onto the waters. Christine stared at an old black and white photograph of the gigantic pieces of carved glass and traced their etched lines with her finger. It was like magic, the way they could send out long streams of light to guide ships through the fog and stormy weather.

She remembered seeing the light for the first time, sending its rhythmic message over the Charlottetown harbour. Even though she was miserable, the light seemed to reach out to her. Now she couldn't wait to see the source of the light for herself.

She was brought back to reality by the sound of the bell. Christine quickly packed up her knapsack and rushed to meet Jennifer and her mother at the front entrance of the school.

Chapter Seven

MEETING THE McINTOSHES

On the way to the Governors Light, Jennifer and Monica Miller chatted about old houses and good places to shop in Charlottetown. Christine stared out the window, drinking in the scenery. The passing countryside was spotted with patches of red soil, glowing in the late afternoon sunshine. She wondered why she hadn't noticed before how pretty the Island was.

They left Charlottetown and headed along the Trans-Canada highway, heading back towards the Confederation Bridge. About ten minutes outside Charlottetown, they made a left turn and headed back towards the shore.

After winding their way through some large farms, they found the dirt road that would take them to the point of land where the Governors Light stood. It was just a stone's throw across the harbour from Charlottetown but there was no direct way to get to the old lighthouse other than by water.

"There used to be a ferry that ran across from here to Charlottetown," Jennifer told them, after Monica commented about the distance they had travelled.

"My dad says that folks used to come across here in the summer and have family picnics. Then they'd take the ferry back to their homes in downtown Charlottetown."

"It sounds marvellous," Christine's mom exclaimed. "We'll have to try the Wood Islands ferry across the Strait someday. I guess that's the only ferry experience left these days."

"I forgot you came across the bridge from the mainland, not the ferry," Jennifer giggled. "We're still getting used to the thing."

"What was it like before the bridge?" Christine asked, with genuine curiosity.

"Well, we were always speeding to catch the ferry. We grew up knowing that you had to always hurry to catch the boat," Jennifer replied. "And in the summer, especially, there were often huge lineups. All the tourists."

"The people from away," Christine added, remembering how Melanie had called her a CFA

"In the winter, the ferry would sometimes get shut down by the weather and you'd have to wait for days to get across. One time, it even got stuck on a sandbar and everyone was stranded," Jennifer explained.

Christine was quiet in the back seat as her mother and Jennifer continued to chat. Jennifer reminded her in some ways of Allie. She was honest and spoke her mind and she wasn't fake in any way. At least, that was what Allie used to be like before she started worrying about whether Brittany was paying enough attention to her or not.

Christine's mom slowly directed the Jeep along another winding dirt road that was not much more than a pair of tire tracks through the woods. Christine held her breath as they passed through the final row of trees. Suddenly the gigantic structure of the lighthouse loomed over them.

"It's huge," Christine gasped and craned her neck out the window for a better look. The lighthouse was a tapered square tower, with red and white stripes alternating up its sides. Christine had read that the tower was sixty feet tall, and she noticed how it gradually narrowed as it reached towards the sky. Christine could just barely see the top of the lighthouse, as the big glass light was surrounded by a steel balcony. A small two-story house was built onto the back of the main structure.

"It's beautiful," Jennifer said, softly. "I've passed by the lighthouse lots of times on my father's boat, but I've never seen it up close."

Monica waved to an elderly man standing in the doorway of the red and white building.

"Girls, Mr. McIntosh is waiting for us," she urged them out of their reverie.

Mr. McIntosh was a tall, slender man with grey hair. He wore a thick navy cardigan, and Christine noticed a pipe and a bag of tobacco sticking out of one pocket. On his feet, he wore a pair of well-worn rubber boots, caked in the ever-present red mud.

"Welcome to the Governors Light," he said as the girls and Monica walked up to the front step. They shook hands. "Call me Mack," he urged them.

Christine stood, staring up at the giant sloped walls of the old building. Mack gave them a quick history of the light's design.

"The main part of the building sits on a rock foundation. The house is built from some sturdy trees that used to stand here on the shore," he said. "She's a piece of work to paint, she is," Mack added with a chuckle. "Always red and white stripes, painted over and over again."

"That looks like a lot of work!" Monica exclaimed.

Mack nodded. "But there at the top is her reason for being. That light has guided many a ship to safety over the years." He pointed to the flashing light. Christine looked up in wonder at the beam that she had first seen from across the harbour. It flickered mysteriously, as if winking at them down below.

Mack directed them into the building itself. As he welcomed them inside, he pulled off his boots and slipped into a pair of leather slippers.

"It's a bit drafty," he said apologetically. "When the wind blows, the whole thing shakes, she does."

Christine looked around in fascination. The entry room was filled with antiques and old photographs, all in some way associated with the lighthouse. Her eyes were drawn to a gigantic piece of carved glass, sitting in one corner of the room.

"Is that one of the lights?" she asked.

Mack followed Christine's gaze and nodded his head approvingly.

"She's a beauty, isn't she?" he said, walking over to the piece of glass. "We've managed to save almost all the old pieces of the lighthouse from over the years. It wasn't easy. The government was always wanting to just throw them out. Betty did too. But I managed to stash them away. The old shed is full of even more, some from other old lighthouses that no longer exist." A cloud came over Mack's face as he was reminded of the sorry fate of the big, old buildings.

"How do you do?" said Betty, as she came into the room, carrying a tray of tea and cookies. The girls and Monica introduced themselves.

"The tea can wait, missus," Mack grinned. "First, I'd like to take these young ladies on a tour."

Christine smiled to herself at the way he said "tour." It was one of the words she had noticed that Islanders pronounced differently. When they said it, the word seemed to rhyme with "floor" or "snore." When she said tour, it sounded more like "poor." She had also noticed that people on the Island had some very funny ways of describing the weather. It wasn't slippery on the roads — it was "slippy." And a bad weather day was called "dirty." Christine found that she sometimes struggled to understand some of the Islanders she met, even Jennifer. The old lightkeeper had one of the thickest accents she had heard yet, so she hung on his every word. She didn't want to miss anything that he had to say about his beloved lighthouse.

Christine repeated the word "tour" to herself under her breath, stifling a giggle. She followed Jennifer and her mother out of the entry room and into a tiny kitchen. In the centre was a big old white enamel stove, heated with wood.

"What a beauty," Monica said, stroking the old stove. Mrs. McIntosh smiled.

"It takes a special touch to use it, dear, and believe me, when the wind's blowing the wrong way, my bread won't rise. But I've perfected it over the forty-five years that we've been living here," she replied.

Mack gestured for them to follow him up a steep set of stairs that ran out of the back of the kitchen.

"Watch yer step," he cautioned.

As they reached the second floor, Christine noticed that the rooms were narrower, following the tapering lines of the lighthouse itself. There were two bedrooms, each filled with antiques.

"What a view!" Jennifer gasped, gazing out one of the windows.

"Aye, that's nothing yet," Mack answered, winking. They followed him up another steep set of stairs to an alcove with a woodstove, a big armchair, a desk and a bookshelf.

"This is where I spend most of my time," he told them. He pointed to the old desk. "That's where I used to keep the logs, when the lighthouse was operational," he explained. "I've kept all the records from over the years."

He pulled out a thick ledger from the bookshelf, labelled 1952. "This was the first year we lived here," he said, his eyes watering over with the memory. "Of course, that wasn't my first time in a lighthouse. I took over my father's posting at North Cape after the war. But when Betty and I got married, I got the plum assignment here at the Governors Light."

"Your father was a lightkeeper?" Christine asked.

"Aye, and his father and grandfather before him. The McIntoshes have been tending lights as long as they've been here on Prince Edward Island."

"What happened when they automated the lighthouse?" Monica asked quietly.

"I was near sixty anyway," Mack said, shaking his head. "I took early retirement on the condition that we got to stay here in the lighthouse. It's been a good arrangement until now."

"Did you sign a deal then? I mean, if it's on paper, they can't kick you out," Christine said eagerly.

"No," he said, sadly. "It was just a gentlemen's agreement that we shook hands on. But now all the government cares about is saving money. They want to get rid of this place entirely, and us too."

"Surely this place has some kind of historical protection?" Monica asked.

"The historical society has been trying to save it for years," Jennifer answered. "My dad has been involved. But the federal government says the building is not safe and it would be too expensive to fix it up."

"They've tried, missus," Mack said. "But it's a done deal. It's just money that matters to them now."

He pulled out a yellowed newspaper clipping. He put on his glasses, cleared his throat and carefully started to read.

The federal government started automating the lighthouses in the 1960s and now all the lights across Prince Edward Island are run by machines, not humans. The Governors Light was one of the last to be automated in the mid-1980s.

It's a matter of economics, one federal bureaucrat said. He pointed out that the Coast Guard could save three million dollars by getting rid of lightkeepers.

"And so, they shut 'er down," Mack concluded. "The lives we could save just weren't worth the money any more."

Christine shuddered at the cold calculation of the worthiness of the lightkeeper's work. There was a pause as Mack took off his glasses. As they watched in silence, he carefully folded up the newspaper article and put it away. Then, he pointed to a metal ring hanging from the ceiling.

"Now we move on to the best part of our tour," Mack said. Christine held her breath. It was time to see the light.

Chapter Eight

THE LIGHT UP CLOSE

*C*hristine looked up eagerly as Mack pulled down the trapdoor and anchored it to the wall. On the other side of the door was a set of wooden stairs, with a rope on either side for railing. As the girls and Mrs. Miller followed him carefully up the stairs, they emerged into the glass room, with the light itself in the centre.

"Wow," Christine gasped.

"This is incredible," Jennifer echoed.

"Don't get too close to the light," Mack warned. "She gets good and hot."

They followed him around the narrow space surrounding the light. All around them were the glass windows and a spectacular view of the Charlottetown cityscape on one side and the Northumberland Strait on the other.

"Need some air?" Mack asked. He pointed to a square hinged door under one of the windows, leading outside. The girls and Monica crawled through the hatch to get out onto the iron balcony that circled the glass room.

The sun hung just above the horizon. The sky still had streaks of red and orange that reached like fingers over the rolling green hills and the dark blue waves. Behind them, the light sent out its pulsing message across the land and water.

"Over there is Governors Island," Mack said, pointing off to a tiny piece of land out in the strait. "It was named for the first governor of the Island when it was part of France. Seems the governor's ship ran into a nor-easter coming out of the harbour and ran aground on the island. That's why this here light came in handy. The waters can get mighty shallow around here."

There was a chill in the air as Christine looked across the harbour to the boardwalk where she had stood when she first saw the light. Then, the lighthouse seemed tiny and the flash of light so thin. Up close, the light was enormous, powerful enough to cut through thick fog and driving snow. Gripping the iron railing, Christine closed her eyes and the smell of the salt and sand drifted up to where they stood. If she stood very still, she could feel the mechanical motion of the light making its circle, over and over again. The vibration of the revolving light was regular and constant, like a panting animal.

"She's magical, she is," Mack murmured, breaking their silence. Looking at her mother and Jennifer, Christine knew that they too had felt the magic of the lighthouse.

"We'd best be getting down, or Betty'll have my head." He chuckled, as he carefully led the girls and Monica back through the door under the railing, pulling the latch closed behind them.

Over tea, Christine and Jennifer explained the purpose of their visit.

"What can we do to help?" Jennifer asked.

"What do you mean help, dear? I thought you were going to write a report about the lighthouse," Betty said.

"We are," Christine answered. "But we would also like to do something to help fight what the government is doing to you. It just doesn't seem fair."

The McIntoshes looked confused. Christine felt her heart sink. They probably think we're just kids, she thought. And even worse, I'm a kid from away.

"Couldn't the girls get involved with the historical society?" Monica suggested, sensing a hesitation from the older couple.

"I don't know how much more they can do," Mack said shaking his head. "We're supposed to move out December first, and the demolition is scheduled for the spring."

"Have they tried a petition? What about letters to the minister?" Christine proposed.

"Well, no," Mack replied.

"That's a great idea," Jennifer piped in. "A letter-writing campaign to save the lighthouse."

"We've got a computer and photocopier the girls can use," Monica said.

"That's very kind of you girls but I don't want you to be disappointed," Betty said, offering them another cookie.

"It's worth a shot, missus," Mack interjected. "Is there anything you need?" he asked Jennifer.

"Some old photographs might help," Jennifer replied.

Mack stood up and turned to go upstairs to pick some out. Christine noticed that the old man swayed slightly as he got up from his rocking chair. Betty gave him a worried look and her gaze followed him out the door.

"He just can't imagine living anywhere but a lighthouse," Betty said, after her husband left the room. "He finds it hard to admit that he's the end of the line for the McIntosh family. Our son is a computer programmer in Toronto and our daughter lives in Calgary with her husband. So the McIntoshes are moving away from the sea."

"What about your family?" Christine asked.

"They're sea-going people too," she replied. "My father was a fisherman all his life. I've always lived by the sea."

"Where would you go? I mean, if you had to leave," Jennifer posed the question carefully.

"My daughter wants us to move out to Alberta with her. But that's out of the question. I guess we'd find a small place somewhere on the shore." Betty sighed.

"Then there's all the stuff he's collected," she added, sadly. "It has been his life's work, preserving the history of the lighthouse. But no one seems to want it."

"Isn't there a museum or gallery that could take it?" Monica inquired.

"Oh, they'll take a piece or two but not all of it," Betty explained.

Mack returned with a handful of photos that he handed to Christine. On top was a black and white photo of a young couple on their wedding day, standing with the Governors Light in the background.

"You were married here?" Christine said surprised.

"Aye," he answered, smiling at his wife. "We've many fond memories of this place."

Everyone was silent for a moment, staring at the old photograph.

"Well, we had better get going. It was lovely to meet you," Monica said, standing up and ushering the girls to the door.

"Good luck with your project," Betty called as they left.

"And come back any time," her husband added. The girls waved as the Jeep pulled out of the driveway, heading back through the darkness to Charlottetown.

On the way home, the girls and Monica talked about their plans.

"They're a lovely couple," Monica remarked. "It would be such a shame if they had to move."

"And how could they even think about tearing that place down?" Christine interjected. "It's ... it's magic. The harbour wouldn't be the same without that lighthouse."

"Yes, we Islanders sometimes take things too much for granted," Jennifer said, thoughtfully. "My dad has been involved with the Heritage committee for years. They fight and they fight, but the historic buildings keep getting torn down. It's a shame, it is."

"I can't believe that in such a wonderful, historical place, people would allow buildings to be torn down," Monica commented.

"That's just the way it is," Jennifer replied.

"Well, that's not going to happen this time," Christine said.

As they continued the drive back to Charlottetown, Christine suddenly thought about her friends back in Toronto. What would they be doing right now? Probably at the bagel shop or hanging out at Brittany's house. Christine felt guilty as she realized that this was the first time she had thought about them all day.

Chapter Nine

A LIFE FAR AWAY

*T*he next day was Saturday, and Jennifer came over to Christine's house in the afternoon. She had spent the morning helping her dad at the fish market and she brought a bag full of mussels for the Millers. She shyly offered them to Monica.

"We've never cooked these ourselves before," Monica smiled, apologetically.

"All you need is an onion and a can of tomatoes. My dad uses basil and garlic. Oh, and his secret ingredient." Jennifer smiled.

"And that is?" Christine asked, nudging her friend.

"Well, you are 'from away.' How do I know that the secret is safe with you?" she teased.

"And the secret ingredient is?" Christine wagged her finger at her friend.

"Okay, okay. Just a few hot chili flakes. But you didn't hear it from me!"

The girls sat at the counter, watching, as Monica followed Jennifer's directions. Monica cooked up a spicy sauce for the mussels, boiling them in a huge, steaming pot for five minutes.

Soon the kitchen was filled with a tantalizing mix of spices and seafood smells. When the mussels were done, the Millers gathered around the kitchen table, helping themselves to the steaming shellfish.

"These are delicious," Christine said, surprised. "I didn't think I would like them but I do." She wiped off her fingers, after tossing her fifth mussel shell onto the growing pile.

"You seem to be changing your mind about a lot of things," her dad said, gently ribbing his daughter. "How's the letter-writing campaign coming?"

"We're just starting to design the letter and petition," Christine explained.

"I'm glad to see the computer being put to such good use," Rob said.

"Oh, by the way, Christine," Monica broke into the conversation as she collected the platters of empty mussel shells. "There was a message on the machine this morning from Allie."

Christine was startled. Why Allie was calling her? Then she remembered their last conversation and felt confused. She had been so sure then that she wanted to move back to Ontario.

"Do you want to call your friend before we get started? I don't mind," Jennifer suggested.

"Nah, she's a real windbag. I'll be on the phone forever," Christine replied, then felt guilty for speaking badly about her friend. "Let's get this done," she said, brushing Allie and her other problems out of her mind.

"Hey, look at this!" Christine exclaimed, waving one of the local history books that Jennifer had brought over. "It explains all the names of places across the Island. Here's Governors Island. 'Named for Robert David Gotteville de Belile, appointed governor of Ile Saint-Jean 1720.' Then, it was called Ile Gouverneur. In 1765, it became Governors Island. And the Mi'kmaq call it Okosik, which means place where goods are landed."

"Except, in the case of the Governor, he didn't really mean to land there." Jennifer giggled.

For the next couple of hours, the girls sat at the computer, working out the perfect wording for their petition. They also put together a letter that people could sign and send to Ottawa to lobby for the Governors Lighthouse.

"Did you ask your dad about what the historical society is going to do?" Christine asked, as they waited for the printer to spit out a sample copy of their petition.

"He said that they got nowhere talking to the Coast Guard people here and the Island Members of Parliament just didn't seem very interested," Jennifer replied. "Now the society is busy trying to save a historic building here in the downtown, so they've given up for a while on the lighthouse."

"But they're going to kick the McIntoshes out on December first."

"I know, but they're going to tear down this house in two weeks. So they say it's more urgent." Jennifer shrugged.

"But your dad thinks the lighthouse can be saved?"

Jennifer nodded. "The government says it would take half a million to fix her up. But my dad says he knows some fellows around town who could do it for next to nothing. They'd donate their time and all we'd need to buy is the wood."

The girls were quiet as they read over the rough draft of their petition.

We urge the federal government to preserve the historic Governors Lighthouse. It is an important landmark on the Charlottetown harbour. We also ask the government to honour its promise to Dave and Betty McIntosh, who were told they could live in the lighthouse as long as they desired.

"What do you think?" Christine asked.

"I think it's good," Jennifer replied. Then she added in a soft voice, "Do you really think we can do this?"

Christine nodded, determinedly.

"You're so confident," Jennifer marvelled. "That must come from growing up in a big city."

Christine looked surprised. "I think you're the one who's got it all together," she answered. "You're the one on the volleyball team, with all the friends at school and good marks. You're much more confident than I am."

Jennifer laughed. "Well, then, I guess we're just the ones for the job then. The federal government has met its match in the two of us."

"Melanie and Ashley don't think so," Christine said, her smile fading.

"What do you mean?"

"Oh, you know. They think I'm just a snob from away."

Jennifer shook her head. "People make a big joke out of the come from away thing. But it's really not such a big deal. Really."

"But they do think I'm a snob, don't they?"

Jennifer paused. "Maybe you were a bit snobbish the first couple of days of school. I wouldn't worry about it." Jennifer gave Christine a reassuring smile and continued packing up the petitions.

Later that afternoon, after Jennifer left, Christine went downstairs. Her father was sitting in front of the TV watching a football game.

"What's up, Chrissie?" he asked, seeing the pensive look on his daughter's face.

"Why didn't you like my friends in Toronto?" she asked bluntly.

Her father looked surprised. "What gives you that idea?" he said, concern spreading across his face.

"I heard what you said to Mom. You said my friends were snobs and I was going to become one too."

"Oh, Chrissie, I'm sorry," her father replied, apologetically. "I didn't mean for you to hear that."

"But you meant it, didn't you?" Christine persisted.

Her father paused for a moment to gather his thoughts. "I guess it wasn't Allie or Brittany that I minded so much as the influence they had on you. You seemed like a different person when you were with them."

His voice faded off. "It's not about you, Chrissie," he continued finally. "Maybe it's me. Maybe I'm the one who never felt as though I fit in, that I would never make enough money or have the right car or a big enough house."

"You didn't have to worry about that stuff," Christine said, eager to continue the conversation. "Brittany can act like a snob sometimes. I just got used to it. But Allie's not that bad."

"I worried that you were going to want all the things that they had. And I couldn't give them to you," her father said wistfully. "But things like that don't seem to matter as much here. The people here are more like the people that I grew up with. It's who you are not what you have that really matters. That's what I like about it."

"Allie and I are like that too. And with Brittany, it's more of a show really. She's just worried about impressing people all the time," Christine explained. For some reason, she felt she had to defend her old friends, even if they had deserted her.

"But, Chrissie, why should she care what other people think? That's just what I'm talking about."

"But everyone's like that. Right?"

"Only if you choose to live your life that way. And I don't any more. I'm tired of trying to have the biggest house or the biggest car." Her father frowned. "I hope that doesn't disappoint you."

"Dad, you're not listening to me. I don't care. But I don't think you're being fair to my friends."

"I think we should just agree to disagree on Allie and Brittany," Rob suggested. Christine nodded, eager to make peace with her father. At the same time, she felt a nagging guilt that she had somehow let her friends down.

"By the way, I put up the birdhouse this afternoon," Rob said. He pointed out the window. "You can see it perfectly from the kitchen. See. Over there, just behind the lilac tree."

"You fixed it!" Christine exclaimed, embarrassed as she remembered how she had broken the birdhouse just before they left Toronto. "It looks great."

She and her father turned their attention back to the TV screen, and Rob passed Christine a bowl of popcorn. They munched away contentedly, commenting every once in a while on the game. Christine couldn't remember the last time she and her dad had watched TV together, but she knew that it had been a very long time.

Chapter Ten

THE INVITATION

*M*onday and Tuesday, Christine and Jennifer spent hours after school, distributing petitions to stores and schools around Charlottetown. Monica happily chauffeured them around and even spent hours on her own in the library, doing research into the historical significance of the lighthouse.

"Did you know that there are only two remaining lighthouses of this kind in Atlantic Canada?" she said, Tuesday night over supper. "Many of the wooden lighthouses haven't survived," she explained. "It's not that they weren't well built. They just haven't been maintained, and so over the years the government has often chosen to tear them down rather than put money into repairing them. One article I found said that fifty of them were torn down in the 1970s across the Maritimes."

"It sounds as though you've found a real treasure," Rob said. "By the way, I forgot to tell you two," he said suddenly. "The federal Minister of Heritage is coming to the Island next weekend. She's going to be attending a meeting at the Confederation Centre. My boss is on the board there and mentioned it to me."

Christine's eyes lit up. "Yes! This is our big chance," she said, springing up from the table. "I've got to phone Jennifer and tell her." As she left the room, Christine did a little dance, grinning at her parents.

Christine dashed to the phone. Just as she was about to pick it up, it rang.

"Chrissie, it's me," the voice whispered. "Can you talk?"

"Allie?" Christine queried. "Why are you whispering?"

"I thought you weren't allowed to talk to us. That's why you didn't call me back, right?" Allie answered, still keeping her voice down.

"Oh, I'm sorry," Christine apologized, a wave of guilt sweeping over her. "I, uh, just didn't have time. Of course, I can talk to you."

"I thought your dad told you that you couldn't?" Allie continued, sounding confused.

"Oh, that's old news," Christine shrugged. "We're getting along much better now."

"Oh, really," Allie said, still not quite sure what was going on.

"What's new?" Christine asked, trying to change the subject.

"Have we got a surprise for you!" Allie gushed. "You're going to get a package tomorrow and guess what's in it?"

Christine giggled. "If I knew, Allie, then it wouldn't be a surprise."

"Right. Well, I'll tell you anyway. Brittany's parents have given her some of their bonus points and she's sending you a ticket to come here next Saturday," Allie squealed.

Christine was shocked.

"It's Brittany's fourteenth birthday, remember?" Allie continued. "We're having a huge party. Everyone will be here, including you!"

"I don't know what to say," Christine stammered.

"You had better be a bit more excited when Brittany calls," Allie teasingly reprimanded her friend for her lack of enthusiasm.

"I mean, I'm thrilled," Christine stumbled over her words, not even knowing what she was saying. "I just didn't expect something like this. I didn't think … I guess I thought you guys had forgotten me."

"Of course not," Allie replied. "So we'll see you next Saturday. Bye now."

Christine was standing, the phone still in her hand, when her mother came into the kitchen.

"What did Jennifer have to say?" her mother asked.

"Huh?" Christine said.

"Was she excited about the Heritage Minister?" Monica repeated, confused by her daughter's reaction.

"Uh, yeah. I mean, I guess so," Christine stammered. "I've got to go do some work on the computer. Can I load the dishwasher later?"

Up in her room, Christine lay on her bed, staring at a framed photo of herself, Allie and Brittany. Her best friends looked suddenly so unfamiliar. So much had happened in the three weeks since she had left Toronto.

Christine was startled by a knock on the door.

"Can I come in?" Jennifer asked.

She was carrying a knapsack, stuffed full of letters and petitions. She waved a poster in front of Christine and grinned.

"Look at this. The Minister of Heritage is coming here. My dad says she's the one who makes decisions about heritage stuff, like the lighthouse. She's going to be giving a public lecture. Here! Next week!" Jennifer said, spinning around the room in excitement. Christine stared blankly at her friend, not reacting.

"This is our chance to make her listen to us," Jennifer continued, still not noticing Christine's lack of response. Suddenly Jennifer stopped and looked at her friend. "What's the matter? You don't seem very excited."

Christine thought for a minute about taking Jennifer into her confidence. But she wasn't sure her new friend would understand her dilemma. As far as Jennifer was concerned, Christine didn't even talk to her friends in Toronto. And Jennifer had no idea that Christine still harboured a dream of moving back there.

"So, what are we going to do?" Christine tried to focus her attention back on the lighthouse project.

"I think we need to get a bunch of supporters of the lighthouse out to that meeting. I can round up some kids from school and I'll get my dad to spread the word to the historical society," Jennifer suggested, jotting down some names in her notebook.

"What can I do?" Christine asked.

"You'll have to ask the Minister about the lighthouse," Jennifer replied.

"Why me? What about the McIntoshes?" Christine said, flustered.

"They can't do it because that would seem as if they're just doing it for themselves," Jennifer shook her head. "If you do it, you can argue the historical significance of the lighthouse *and* saving the McIntosh's home. Besides, the reporters will love it. I can just see the headlines now: 'High school student pleads for local lighthouse.'"

Christine still wasn't convinced. "Why can't you do it? You live here."

"You live here now too," Jennifer answered stubbornly. "You're a great public speaker and I'm sure you've done more of this kind of thing than I have."

Christine raised her eyebrows. "I don't think so," she replied. "And besides, I don't think that a person from away should be doing it. I'm just a snob from Toronto, remember? Ask Melanie and Ashley."

Christine immediately felt herself blushing at her own words. She thought about the free ticket to Toronto that was about to arrive at her house and the extravagant birthday party that her friends were planning.

Jennifer looked as if she was about to answer, but Christine interrupted her, waving her hands. "We'll decide later," she said suddenly. "Let's just get to work."

That weekend, Christine and Jennifer spent all their spare time getting ready for the public meeting. On Monday, they put up posters around Queen Charlotte and after school they went around town to pick up the pages of completed petitions. The girls grinned with pleasure as they saw the growing public support for their idea of saving the lighthouse.

Christine made sure she was the first one to the mailbox Monday morning and managed to hide the package from Brittany before her parents saw it. She still hadn't called her friends in Toronto. Whenever the phone rang, she ran to answer it. She couldn't risk Allie or Brittany mentioning anything to her parents. At the same time, she didn't want to call her friends herself because she didn't know how to explain why she wasn't coming.

On Thursday morning, just as Christine was rushing out the door to school, the phone rang. It was Brittany.

"Hey, babe, you all set for the big party Saturday night? You did get the package didn't you?" Brittany teased her.

"Yeah. I mean, thanks a lot Brittany, but ..." Christine started to explain.

"No buts. Martin and I will come to the airport to get you. And then we're going shopping in the afternoon. On me," Brittany continued, not letting Christine finish her sentence. "Then, Saturday night, my house. The biggest birthday bash in the history of North Park High school. And, Chrissie, my parents say that you can stay as long as you want," Brittany added.

Christine was silent.

"You know, like live here. That's what you wanted, wasn't it?" Brittany said, suddenly serious.

"It was. I mean, sure. But I have to get back here on Sunday actually. For school, you know," Christine explained.

"I thought you'd just switch to North Park," Brittany replied.

"I don't want to lose the term. Maybe after Christmas," Christine blurted out, realizing she was digging herself deeper and deeper into the lie.

"Well, the important part is that you'll be here for my birthday," Brittany concluded. "See you at the airport!"

After she hung up the phone, Christine pictured herself arriving at the airport, getting a big hug from Brittany and Allie. All of a sudden, she wasn't sure what she wanted to do.

She could ask her parents if she could go, but she was sure that they wouldn't let her. For one thing, they would never let her accept a free ticket, especially from Brittany. She didn't want to provoke another huge battle with them. They were so keen on getting her settled into her new life in Charlottetown, leaving her old life in Toronto behind her.

Suddenly Christine felt the old anger stirring inside her. She remembered the stares of everyone at school the first day she arrived and the whispers in the hallways. She thought about what Melanie and Ashley had said about her. Her parents said it was only a matter of time before she fit in. But what if she could never fit in here no matter how long she stayed or how hard she tried?

Maybe her parents were wrong. Maybe she did belong in Toronto after all. At the very least she needed to go back and see her friends. Her parents wouldn't even need to know. That way, there would be no fight. Christine felt a surge of nervous excitement at the thought of sneaking away to Toronto to see her friends. Then she could decide if that was really where she wanted to live. She owed her friends that much.

"Maybe I can do both," Christine mumbled to herself as she ran up the steps of Queen Charlotte. "As long as I'm back here on Sunday, nobody will mind."

Chapter Eleven

TALES OF THE OLD SALT

*T*hat evening, Rob drove Christine and Jennifer out to the Governors Light. He was eager to get a look at the landmark that had so inspired his wife and daughter. The McIntoshes greeted the girls warmly. Mack gave Rob's hand a vigorous handshake and slapped him on the back.

"That's a fine daughter you've got there," he said, as Christine blushed. "She's got quite a way with the words, even for someone from away." He added a wink in Christine's direction.

"You girls have taken on a mighty load of work," Betty added, as she got them settled in the parlour with tea and sweets.

"What we really need now is for the two of you to come to the Confederation Centre on Sunday night to face the Minister," Jennifer said.

"It will make it more personal if she sees you," Christine added.

"Christine will make a presentation to the Minister and ask her to designate the building a national historic site," Jennifer continued, smiling encouragingly at her friend. Christine felt a wave of embarrassment as she thought about letting her friend down. But she pushed those thoughts from her mind and averted her eyes as she pulled a notebook out of her knapsack.

There was a knock at the door. Mack sprang to his feet and rushed to the door. "There's someone I want you girls to meet," he shouted over his shoulder. The girls exchanged confused looks.

Mack returned followed by a stocky old fellow with a bushy white beard and a jaunty sailor's hat. He was wearing a thick woollen sweater and knitted socks. He grinned from ear to ear as he was introduced to Christine and Jennifer.

"This is the Old Salt," Mack explained. "He's a man of the sea and knows almost as much about the history of the light-houses as I do." He said the last part with a wink, nudging the Old Salt, who let out a loud guffaw.

"And this is me dog, Marco Polo," the old sailor added, pointing to a bushy-haired Sheltie that followed his every step. Marco dropped to the floor as the Old Salt settled into the rocking chair by the woodstove. Christine thought it was an unusual name for a dog but didn't dare ask more about it. Why would the dog be named after an explorer?

She had to hold back a giggle at the old Islander's thick accent. He told them he was from "out Souris way."

"I was born within spitting distance of East Point," he explained. "She's the furthest point of land on the eastern shore of our fine island."

"Were you a lightkeeper too?" Jennifer asked politely.

"Nay, but I fished for my livelihood," he replied, slowly sipping the tea that Betty had handed him. Once she was out of the room, he drew a flask out of his jacket pocket and with a wink, poured an amber liquid into his tea. Grinning, he toasted the two girls and Mack, who shook his head with a laugh.

"The lights have been good to us fishermen," the Old Salt continued. "But there have still been many lives lost off of our P.E. Island."

The Old Salt stared for a moment at the flames flickering behind the glass door of the woodstove. Christine shivered and imagined icy ocean waters and the dramatic sight of the old mighty ships torn apart by the pounding waves.

"And the mightiest shipwreck of them all" — the Old Salt paused for emphasis — "was the wreck of the MARCO POLO."

The girls' eyes grew wide as they sensed the old man was getting warmed up to start a story. They pulled their chairs closer. The Old Salt took another sip from his cup.

The MARCO POLO, he told them, was built in 1851 in Saint John, New Brunswick, and she soon gained a reputation as the fastest ship in the world.

"She was a beauty, she was," the Old Salt continued. "She had ceilings of maple paneling and stained glass, the likes you've never seen. And she could make the trip from Australia in less than six months."

Noticing the girls' raised eyebrows, Mack interjected. "That was fast for those days. It was a new record."

Christine glanced over in her father's direction. He was leaning forward, enraptured by the old sailor's story. He gave her a wink.

The Old Salt continued his tale of the MARCO POLO. "The year was 1883. It was July 25th and a mighty storm was brewing. She was carrying a cargo of lumber from Quebec to London when she ran aground at Cavendish," he explained. "She was seen heading to shore at a mighty clip. The crew tried to drop her sails but it was too late. They cut the rigging just as she struck."

Jennifer gasped.

"On the beach the people of Cavendish watched in horror. There was nothing they could do to help as long as the storm continued. Finally they made a huge sign, telling the crew to stay on board until the storm calmed down," the Old Salt continued.

In her mind, Christine pictured the scene. She and her parents had driven up to the white, sandy beaches of Cavendish, now one of the biggest tourist attractions on the Island. She imagined the residents, the women in long dresses, whipped by the turbulent winds, watching in horror as the famous ship floundered just off the shore.

"And she was filled with treasure, b'y, was she not?" Mack interrupted.

"Aye, she was," the Old Salt nodded. "They say that ten thousand dollars in copper and coin and goods were lost. And the fine wood carvings and brass and stained glass, they all washed up on shore in pieces. The ship herself — she broke up and sank right there before their eyes. The fastest ship in the world. Returned home to find a resting place, some say."

"Did people die?" Christine asked, almost afraid to hear the answer.

"Thankfully, no lives were lost, that time at least," the Old Salt replied. "The people of Cavendish showed great hospitality to the crew of the MARCO POLO and took them into their homes."

"Aye, but the Yankee Gale was a much worse storm," Mack jumped in.

"That was a real tragedy," the Old Salt nodded gravely. "But that's a tale for another day."

"Yes, you old fools," Betty reprimanded the two older men. "These girls have to go to school tomorrow. And you sit here regaling them with stories of ancient shipwrecks. What they need is some help with their project." And with that, she shooed Mack up the stairs to find the pictures that the girls had requested. He motioned for Christine to follow. Jennifer, meanwhile, had pulled out a notebook and was asking the Old Salt some questions about other lighthouses he had visited.

Chapter Twelve

THE PULSE OF THE LIGHT

*M*ack ushered Christine upstairs to the alcove. As he flipped through some of his old log books, Christine noticed that the old man wheezed slightly, winded from the exertion of climbing the steep stairs.

"Did you want some of these photos as well?" he asked, thumbing through a thick pile of old black and white pictures.

"Are you sure you don't mind? I mean, this is valuable stuff," Christine protested.

"It will be well worth it if you can save her," he said. Mack pulled down the staircase leading up to the balcony. He pointed up to where the light flickered. "I do my best thinking up there." He winked and motioned for her to follow him up the stairs. Together, they climbed out onto the iron deck, overlooking the harbour.

Above the lighthouse, the first stars of the evening flickered in the sky but their light was muted, compared to the unrelenting gaze of the pulsing beam. Christine drew her coat closer, chilled by the autumn air. Still, she felt safe and somehow at peace, so close to the signalling light.

"She's like a heartbeat," Mack said in a hushed voice.

Christine looked at him in surprise. She realized that the rhythmic pulse of the light was soothing for exactly that reason.

"I've seen the sun rise from the cliffs and the moonlight dance on the waves," the old man continued, staring off into the distance. "We were the lifeline for all the ships that passed by here. Oh, the waters here aren't as dangerous as some spots. But many a captain told me that he breathed easier just knowing that we were here."

"Did you ever have to rescue anyone?" Christine asked.

"There was the odd mechanical breakdown and a ship had to be towed into harbour. And one or two men drowned while we were operational," he responded. "Nothing we could do for them. Just fell overboard and were lost.

"The drownings were the worst," Mack recalled, a frown crossing over his face. "Many times, the tide would take the body out of the harbour and it would take weeks or months before it washed ashore."

Christine shuddered.

"Aye, it's part of living by the sea, lassie," he added, sensing her reaction. "She's magical and powerful and you must always respect her. At least, I always have."

As they stood in silence, Christine mulled over what the old lightkeeper had said. She too felt the tug of the ocean's power, even after living only a short time on the Island, but she felt silly mentioning it.

"It's so beautiful," she said finally.

"I think you do truly understand," Mack answered and she noticed that his wrinkled blue eyes were watery with tears. She wondered if he was thinking about his own children who had turned their backs on this life by the sea. Christine couldn't imagine living here and not feeling the power of the light and the water. She stared out over the black waves and watched the moon dancing in and out of the clouds.

After a momentary pause, he moved back towards the doorway to the lighthouse and Christine reluctantly followed him.

On the way home, Rob drove along with a relaxed smile on his face.

"I see now why you and your mother are so smitten with this lighthouse," he said, turning to his daughter. "And the McIntoshes are super people. Real Islanders."

"It makes me mad that they have to go through all of this," Christine said, a slight edge in her voice. "It's bad enough that they took away his job, but to take away his home too ..."

"I can relate," Rob murmured thoughtfully.

Christine suddenly realized that her father could probably understand, more than anyone, what Mack had gone through. They had both lost their jobs for reasons beyond their control. Christine looked at Jennifer to see if her friend had realized what Christine's dad was talking about.

Rob continued. "You know, all the so-called experts tell you that you will change jobs four or five times in your career. Still, when they come and tell you they don't want you any more, it hits you hard. I just didn't see it coming."

"That was their loss, Dad," Christine replied defensively. She was surprised at her father's honesty, especially with Jennifer in the Jeep. She didn't remember him ever talking like this when they were back in Toronto.

"I guess that's one thing you avoid here, at least. The old corporate downsizing trend hasn't hit PEI, has it?" Rob said jokingly, turning to Jennifer.

"No, it's the same here, maybe even worse," Jennifer replied, in a serious tone. "The farmers are having a tough time. And the fishery has taken a big hit. My dad just couldn't afford to keep fishing. And the big companies don't even consider coming here. So young people have to go away. They call it the PEI brain drain."

Christine looked at her friend with surprise. Usually, Jennifer was so happy-go-lucky.

"Will you have to go away?" she asked softly.

"Maybe," Jennifer replied, shrugging her shoulders. "I'd like to go into physiotherapy and they don't offer the program at UPEI. So I'd have to go away to school. Then, there are only a handful of jobs to come back to."

The girls fell into silence, both lost in their own thoughts. As she stared out the window, Christine was suddenly embarrassed by her own lack of direction. Obviously Jennifer had already given a lot more thought to her future than Christine and her friends had. They had all taken it for granted that they would go away to university together. But any conversations about their plans were more focused on how great the parties would be and whether they would live on or off campus.

Christine wasn't even sure what she wanted to study at university. But working on this project was starting to give her some ideas. Maybe journalism, or something to do with public service, she mused. She liked the idea of being able to make a difference.

She thought back to what it felt like standing on the balcony in the darkness. She had never felt as strongly about something as she did about saving the lighthouse. Once the lighthouse was safe, she could go back to Ontario in peace.

Chapter Thirteen

CHRISTINE'S CHOICE

On Friday, Christine squirmed restlessly in her seat in Social Studies class, her mind racing. The reality of her deception was starting to sink in, and she realized she was going to have to get Jennifer to help her out.

As they sat together in the cafeteria eating lunch, Christine tried to think of a way to broach the subject. Jennifer's hair was pulled back in a ponytail, signaling that she was hard at work. She wrinkled the freckles on her nose and squinted her green eyes intently as she bent over a notebook, checking off items on a long list of things to do before the protest on Sunday night.

"We should be able to get the signs made after school. I've got about a dozen people coming out to help, and they've all promised to be at the Centre on Sunday," Jennifer explained. She stopped suddenly and looked carefully at Christine. "What's the matter? You're not even listening."

"I've got a problem. With this weekend," Christine replied, not quite sure where to start. "My friends in Toronto have sent me a plane ticket. It's Brittany's fourteenth birthday tomorrow and I, uh, promised I'd go. But my parents don't know."

"But you can't go this weekend!" Jennifer gasped.

"Wait. There's more. I need to tell my mom and dad that I'll be at your house for the weekend." Christine stumbled through her explanation, watching the colour drain from Jennifer's face.

Jennifer sat silently, twisting her pen in her hand, not able to look Christine in the eyes.

"I'll be back Sunday afternoon in lots of time for the Minister's speech," Christine added quickly. Jennifer's expression didn't change.

"I guess if it's that important to you, sure," Jennifer said, trying to be sincere. It was obvious, though, that she was hurt by Christine's announcement. Jennifer continued, choosing her words carefully. "I don't like lying to your parents. They've both been so helpful with the project. It just doesn't seem fair. Can't you tell them the truth?"

"Oh, never mind," Christine said, flustered, throwing her dishes onto a tray and getting up from the table. Then, realizing that Jennifer was her only choice, she sat down again.

"It's not that I want to go but I promised my friends," Christine explained. "And my parents don't particularly like my friends. So things would go smoother for me if they just didn't know."

"What about our promise to the McIntoshes? They're counting on us. Isn't that more important than some party?"

"I said I'd be back," Christine retorted, flushed at her friend's accusation.

"Okay, okay, let's get as much done as possible before you go. And, yes, I'll cover for you," Jennifer answered. She got up from the table and left before Christine could even thank her.

Jennifer avoided Christine all afternoon. Christine knew her friend was angry but at the same time she felt suddenly exhilarated at the thought of going back to Toronto. She imagined herself, Allie and Brittany, sipping lattes at the mall, just as they used to. She would have to check out all her favourite stores and she would definitely find something nice to bring back for Jennifer. That would smooth things over, she was sure. Christine still felt bad about lying to her parents but as long as they never found out, it was better than getting into a big battle with them.

After the final bell rang, Christine rushed to their homeroom. Jennifer had asked the vice-principal to make an announcement inviting any interested students to meet to talk about the rally on Sunday. Christine was surprised to see that the room was already crowded by the time she got there. She recognized some kids from her Social Studies class. Some younger students were also clustered at the back of the room. Christine noticed Ashley and Melanie and some of the other volleyball players perched on desks. At the front of the class Jennifer was smiling and talking to Scott MacFarlane, one of the most popular guys in the school.

Christine had noticed Scott before and he had even said hi to her a couple of times. He was definitely cute — over six feet tall, reddish-blonde hair and blue eyes. He was on the honour roll and one of the top local hockey players. Girls were always flirting with him in the hallways and cafeteria but Jennifer had told Christine that he didn't have a steady girlfriend.

"What is he doing here?" Christine muttered to herself. Jennifer was being very friendly with Scott. She felt a sudden surge of jealousy. Christine knew that the guys at school found Jennifer attractive. In contrast, Christine felt like the plain Jane from away.

Jennifer spotted Christine and waved her up to the front. "I need to talk to you," she whispered to Christine.

"We had better get going," Scott said, glancing at his watch. "I've got practice in half an hour."

Jennifer looked flustered. Christine wondered what was bothering her. Maybe she's just nervous in front of Scott, Christine thought.

"Thanks for coming out," Jennifer began the meeting. She gave the group of students a quick history of the lighthouse project and the dilemma that the McIntoshes were facing.

"We basically need two things from all of you," Scott jumped in next, to Christine's surprise. She glanced over at Jennifer, who stared straight ahead. "We're going to make some picket signs here tonight."

Scott continued. "Jennifer and Christine have prepared some captions. On Sunday, we'll meet at six-thirty at the Centre so that we can be picketing when the Minister arrives. Then, during the question period after the Minister's speech, I'm going to ask a question about saving the lighthouse."

Christine couldn't believe what she was hearing. She glared furiously at Jennifer, who refused to even look at her.

"Great work on this project, Christine," Scott said, after he and Jennifer wrapped up the meeting and the students split into groups to get to work on the picket signs. "I'd like to talk to you some more about the lighthouse and stuff. Can I call you this weekend?" Christine noticed that he seemed to blush slightly when he mentioned calling her. But she was too angry to even wonder why.

"I won't be on the Island this weekend," she replied, coldly. "I'm going back to Toronto."

Scott looked surprised. "You're going to be there on Sunday night, aren't you?"

"I don't think I can make it," Christine answered as Jennifer walked up to them.

"You can't make it?" Jennifer hissed. "Or you don't want to make it?"

"Well, you obviously don't need me. You seem to have the whole thing under control," Christine replied.

"I can explain, Christine," Jennifer said. "I wasn't sure you would be back in time so I asked Scott if he would mind asking the question at the meeting."

"You mean, you were supposed to do it?" Scott asked, looking from Jennifer to Christine.

"What's going on?" Melanie asked, coming up to the front of the class.

"We're just trying to decide who's going to ask the Minister the question about the lighthouse," Scott explained. "Apparently Christine is going to do it, if she can make it back from Toronto in time."

Melanie shook her head. "That will never work," she protested. "It has to be someone from here. It can't be some hotshot jetting in from Toronto. How would that look?"

Scott and Jennifer exchanged looks. Christine grabbed her knapsack.

"I can see that you have all the bases covered," she said. "I think I'll just stay a couple of extra days in Toronto. Good luck with the meeting."

Christine stormed out the door with Jennifer chasing after her. To her chagrin, Christine felt hot tears welling up in her eyes as she headed down the stairs of Queen Charlotte.

"Christine, wait," Jennifer pleaded, running down the steps. "Melanie didn't mean it. She's just jealous because she doesn't like the fact that you and I are such good friends. And besides she's after Scott MacFarlane and he seems more interested in you."

"Me? What about you?" Christine answered, pausing to let her friend catch up with her. "You're the one that all the guys are after."

"Nah," Jennifer said, shaking her head. "Scott and I are just friends. We've known each other since elementary school. I'm sorry I didn't get a chance to ask you about getting him involved," Jennifer continued. "You just seemed so distracted by this trip to Toronto. And besides, I knew that we could get lots more kids out if Scott was involved."

"That's okay," Christine said, her eyes still stinging from her tears. "Can I still use you as my alibi?"

"Are you sure you want to go?" Jennifer asked. "I mean, I know they're your friends and everything ..."

"I have to," Christine said stubbornly, though she wasn't so sure herself.

There was a moment of awkward silence.

"Well, I better get back to making those signs," Jennifer said finally.

"I'll see you Sunday afternoon," Christine said.

"You better," Jennifer said. "And, Christine — I hope this party is worth it."

Christine wondered what Jennifer meant. She shrugged her shoulders and headed home to pack.

Chapter Fourteen

ANOTHER THREAT

*W*hen Christine got home, her mother came to greet her at the door. Christine caught her breath: Did her mother know what she was up to?

"Call Mack right away," her mother urged her. "He's very upset."

They hurried into the den and Christine quickly dialled the lightkeeper's number. She wondered if Jennifer had told him that she was going away. How she was ever going to defend her decision to go to Toronto? She looked nervously in her mother's direction as she waited for Mack to answer.

"It's this letter here that I received today from the Coast Guard," the old man explained, and Christine could hear the agitation in his voice. "They say they're going to wreck 'er down at the end of the month."

"What?" Christine said, shocked by his news. "They can't possibly do it that quickly."

"Aye, they can and they will," Mack retorted, a touch of anger in his voice. "According to their records, we've had plenty of warning. They say that they have someone who's interested in the property. Wants to tear down the light and build a hotel or some fool thing."

Christine was silent for a moment, pondering her options. Obviously she couldn't leave now. But her friends were expecting her.

"Mom, can you take me out to the McIntoshes?"

Monica nodded.

"We'll be right there," Christine told Mack.

"I don't know that there's much you can do," the old man muttered but then thanked her before hanging up.

On the way to the lighthouse, Christine stared out the window, feeling even more like a traitor than before. With this renewed threat to the Governors Light, the weekend protest was more important than ever. She had no choice. She had to stay on the Island and skip Brittany's party. She was sure her friends would understand.

Mack was waiting at the door when the Miller's Jeep pulled into the lane. It was already dark, and light flakes of snow were falling. They formed a slushy ice on the waters just off the shore. The light from the beam high above glinted on the whiteness of the snow below.

"Come in and sit down," Betty urged them, taking their coats. The strain of the day's news was etched on her usually cheerful face. She was too distracted even to offer them the usual tea and sweets. She sat down in a chair and watched Monica Miller's face anxiously as she read the letter from the Coast Guard. Monica sighed and handed the letter to Christine.

"It's not good," Monica said, finally. "They have given you ample notice as required. The only thing I can suggest is that we go for an injunction to stop the demolition. That would buy us some time."

"Or maybe it's time to face the inevitable ..." Mack's voice faded off. The old man's face looked almost gray, and Christine noticed that his hands shook slightly as he took the letter back from her mother.

"We may get our answer this weekend," Christine jumped in, shaken by the old man's tone.

"Chrissie, even if the Heritage Minister does agree to consider the case, that could take months," Monica told her daughter. "I think that your dad's firm deals with a lawyer in Charlottetown. Maybe he could draft up some kind of injunction."

"We've no money for any kind of legal battle," Betty said, quietly.

"I'm sure we can find someone who will do it pro bono, at no charge to you," Monica reassured the frail, old woman.

Christine gazed around the cozy sitting room and shuddered. She thought of the couple having to pack up their belongings and leave their beloved lighthouse. She couldn't let that happen.

There was a bang on the door. The Old Salt came in, shaking the snow from his sailor's cap and bending down to brush off Marco Polo. The sailor gingerly pulled off his big snowboots and hung his peacoat on a coathook by the door.

"What's this I hear about more government stupidity?" he said sharply, settling into his usual seat by the fire.

"They're going to pull 'er down," Mack grumbled. "At the end of the month."

The Old Salt shook his head vehemently. "I sense they're in for a bit of a fight first, right, gals?" he asked, turning to Monica and Christine, who both nodded enthusiastically. He got up and stirred the fire, then went to the window and stared outside. "She's startin' to blow," he said finally. "We could be in for a mean nor'easter in the next day or so."

"A nor'easter?" Christine asked.

"When a nor'easter blows, you keep the matches handy, store up on yer milk and supplies and you hunker down till she blows over," Mack said, with a wink.

"It's a dark and dirty night out," the Old Salt said, re-establishing himself in his seat, with Marco Polo at his feet. "What about a ghost story before you head back to town?"

Christine wasn't sure that anyone was in the mood for a story, but she nodded, not wanting to disappoint the old sailor. She hoped that the Old Salt would distract Mack and Betty from their problems, at least for a few minutes.

"This is a story, not of the cruelty of the Mistress Ocean, but of a sailing crew. She was called the FAIRY QUEEN and she plied the waters of the Northumberland Strait," the Old Salt began his story with a flourish of his hand, which still held the poker from the fire. It would have been comic if not for the eerie tone of the old man's voice.

"The incident happened in the year 1853 and 'tis a tragic tale," the Old Salt continued. "She was a steamer, and she left Charlottetown on a Friday forenoon. She was just past Point Prim" — he pointed out the window, south along the Northumberland Strait, — "when the troubles began in heavy seas. She was near Pictou Island when the tiller rope broke."

Christine and her mom stared out the window, following his gaze. The snow was starting to fall harder now, and they could hear the wind whistling against the walls of the lighthouse. The McIntoshes had said that on the stormiest days, they could actually see the wind pushing against the walls of the building. Christine shivered as she imagined the "heavy seas" that would have snapped the rope steering the FAIRY QUEEN.

"Some of the men passengers were handy and they helped the crew splice a makeshift tiller, but the ship, she was in no fine shape. The engineers couldn't get up the steam, even though they broke up part of the deck to burn below," the Old Salt continued. Marco Polo was tilting his head to one side, paying rapt attention to his master's story, which made Christine smile. But her smile soon faded as the story continued.

"There followed one of the most cowardly acts ever committed," he said sadly. "The captain and crew lowered themselves into the boats. Some of the men aboard pleaded with the sailors to come back and take the ladies. But they drifted slowly away."

Christine gasped and her mother looked shocked.

"The passengers continued to bail but she was soon too swamped," the Old Salt continued. "The passengers assembled on the deck of the FAIRY QUEEN. Soon she broke apart, struck by a mighty wave. A few of the men were able to grab onto the upper deck, which broke away and thankfully floated like a raft. They were rescued finally after drifting for eight hours in the storm and the cold."

He stopped for a moment. "The rest were lost. To this day, some say the souls of the lady passengers wander this earth. Their ghostly figures have been seen wandering up into the upper balcony of the old Trinity United Church in Charlottetown."

Christine shivered at the ghostly conclusion of the story. She wondered at the cruelty of the captain and his crew, deserting the passengers and stealing away in the lifeboats. It reminded her of the story of the TITANIC, with lifeboats leaving half-empty, while so many more lives could have been saved.

"A public meeting was held in Charlottetown to examine the cruel and heartless conduct of the captain and his crew," the Old Salt added. "It was said that the captain was haunted by those memories for the rest of his days. And he went to his death, lamenting the horror of that stormy afternoon and the ruthless crew that coerced him into sending those passengers to their watery grave."

Christine and her mother didn't say much on the drive back from the lighthouse. Christine's mother concentrated on the road, which was now getting icy, as the temperature hovered around the freezing mark and the precipitation changed from snow to pelting rain. The weather felt as miserable as Christine did. She planned her conversation with her friends in Toronto. She had to make them understand how important it was for her to be here this weekend.

"Thanks, Mom," Christine said, as they raced into the doorway to get out of the rain.

"Do you want to talk to your dad now?" Monica asked. "Maybe he can make some calls tomorrow about filing that injunction."

"Can we talk about it tomorrow?" Christine suggested. "I, uh, I've got to call Jennifer."

As soon as she closed her door, Christine dialled Brittany's number. No answer. She called Allie's house.

"Allie, it's me," Christine whispered.

"What's up? We're so excited about your trip. Wait until you hear about the party we have planned," Allie said, not even noticing that her friend was whispering.

"That's what I'm calling about," Christine continued. "I can't make it."

"What do you mean?" Allie asked, surprised. "Do you know what Brittany had to go through to get that ticket for you? She had to beg her parents. You know what they're like. You can't be serious. Brittany will kill you."

"I've just got this other thing I have to do," Christine moaned. "It's important."

"It can't wait for a day?" Allie asked. "You'll be home on Sunday. You have to be here for the party. This is important, Chrissie."

Christine remembered the scene earlier at school and how mean the Island girls had been to her. She felt her face growing red as she thought about the way they had dismissed her as someone from away. Even Jennifer had betrayed her by asking Scott to ask the question at the demonstration.

"Oh Allie, let me think about it," Christine relented. "I'll call you in the morning."

"Okay," Allie said, relieved. "And Chrissie —"

"Yeah," Christine answered.

"Don't ever tell Brittany that you weren't going to come," Allie suggested. "You know how she gets. She would definitely take it the wrong way."

After she hung up, Christine took out some clothes and halfheartedly packed them into her knapsack, trying not to look at the pile of petitions on her desk. She kept going over and over the arguments in her mind. The more she thought about what she wanted to do, the more confused she became.

In bed that night, she tossed and turned for hours, occasionally glancing over at the red glowing numbers on her clock radio. Finally, she fell into a troubled sleep. The giant, flashing light appeared, beating in time to the waves crashing up on the shore below. She shuddered as she saw the crumpled bow of a ship. A hand scraped away the sand to reveal the name etched in the side — the FAIRY QUEEN. Nearby was a bloated body, covered in seaweed, washed up on the rocks. In her sleep, Christine walked over to where the body was lying and turned it over. To her horror, she saw her own face looking back up at her. Christine woke up with a start and spent the rest of the night staring at the ceiling, unable to fall back asleep.

Chapter Fifteen

WHERE IS HOME?

The next morning, Christine came into the kitchen as her parents were having their coffee and toast. She was carrying the knapsack full of clothes. She still wasn't sure what she was going to do. Already this morning, she had packed and unpacked her bag. The plane left in an hour. She had to make a decision soon.

"Where are you off to so early on a Saturday morning?" her father teased. Christine felt slightly sick to her stomach as she nervously fingered the straps of her knapsack.

"Uh, Jennifer and I want to get an early start on our work today," she mumbled, heading towards the door.

"Do you need a ride out to the lighthouse?" her mom volunteered. "You girls have to meet with the McIntoshes today, don't you?"

"Jennifer's dad is taking us," Christine lied, wincing slightly. "I'm, uh, going to stay at Jennifer's tonight. Is that okay?"

"Sure thing," her father answered, getting back to his newspaper.

Christine made her way to the door, relieved that the lies were over.

"Are you nervous about tomorrow night?" her father asked, looking up with a smile. "I'm looking forward to hearing your presentation."

Christine looked at him nervously. "Uh, you know what, Dad," she stammered. "I'll be too nervous if you and mom are there. Do you mind?"

Her father looked disappointed but didn't question his daughter. "Good luck then, if we don't see you before," he said, cheerfully.

Just as Christine was about to sneak out the door, her mother came rushing after her. Christine's stomach lurched. She quickly tucked her plane ticket inside the knapsack, hoping her mother hadn't noticed it sticking out from her jacket.

"Chrissie, I talked to your dad about the injunction. He's going to make some calls on it today. He has the home phone numbers of a couple of local lawyers and he thinks he can convince one of them to look into the case for the McIntoshes," her mother said triumphantly. "He'll call you at Jennifer's later and let you know how it's going."

"Uh, no ..." Christine sputtered. "We'll call him. We're going to be running around all day. Tell him I'll call him."

Monica looked puzzled as she closed the door and gave Christine a wave. Christine felt sick to her stomach as she quickly walked towards downtown.

When she got to Queen Street, she noticed a cab sitting outside City Hall. She jumped in. "Can you take me to the airport?" she said breathlessly. The driver nodded and swung the cab around.

When they got to the airport, she paid the driver and quickly made her way to the Air Canada desk. Instead of feeling excited about her trip to Toronto, all she could feel was guilt. She thought about putting on a baseball cap, in case someone from school was at the airport. This is ridiculous, she thought to herself, I feel like an escaped prisoner.

She followed the handful of passengers through the security gate and then out onto the tarmack. She felt a moment of panic as she boarded the tiny plane that would take them to Halifax. But no one paid any attention to her, and slowly, Christine felt her pulse settle.

The tiny plane took off from the Charlottetown airport and flew right over the Governors Light but Christine stubbornly refused to look out the window. She buried her nose in a fashion magazine and envisaged her reunion with her friends in Ontario. After all, she belonged with Allie and Brittany in Toronto. That was home, she told herself over and over again.

The plane trip seemed to last forever as Christine fought off the feelings of guilt that kept passing over her. She felt shaky as she walked through the luggage area at Pearson airport and headed towards the automatic doors leading out to the lobby. She looked around for Allie and Brittany. There was no sign of her friends.

Christine scanned the crowd and then made her way to the pay phones. She scrambled through her purse for a quarter and breathlessly dialled Brittany's number.

"Brittany, it's me. Where are you?" Christine asked as her friend answered.

"Oh, Chrissie, we were just soooo busy. Can you grab a cab?" Brittany urged.

"I guess so," Christine sighed. "What are you up to?" she started to ask, but Brittany had already hung up.

Christine made her way to the taxi stand. She was momentarily startled at how busy the airport was and how big everything seemed. She had to wait fifteen minutes in line for a taxi, and even then a noisy pair of business executives pushed their way into her cab and she had to wait for the next one.

Her heart started pounding harder as she looked out the cab window at the grey sky of the city. The once-familiar trip along the 401 now seemed alien to her, so different from the uncluttered landscape of Prince Edward Island.

Christine stared at her reflection in the window as the cab raced along the busy ten-lane highway. Her hair was slightly longer from when she left and she was dressed the way she would have for a weekend in Toronto: jeans, a Roots sweatshirt, her jean jacket and a pair of sneakers. Still, she felt slightly uncomfortable as she stared at her face in the mirror. How much had changed? Was she different?

When the taxi drew close to Brittany's house, Christine experienced a flurry of mixed emotions. It was good to see the houses and streets of her old neighbourhood. At the same time, she felt another wave of guilt as she thought of her parents, back in Charlottetown, going about their Saturday errands, assuming that Christine was over at Jennifer's house.

Christine felt a surge of frustration as she paid the taxi driver. It was just like Brittany to assume that everyone was made of money, just because her family was.

Brittany's house was the biggest on a street filled with impressive houses. Christine overheard her parents say once that it was worth millions, which had made Christine gasp. Over the years she had known Brittany, she had become used to the house, with its huge staircases, indoor pool and entertainment room. The girls knew they could help themselves to anything in the expansive kitchen with its two stainless steel fridges and the well-stocked cupboards. The housekeeper, Francesca, was usually the only one around when Christine and Allie were over and she made sure the girls had whatever they needed.

Christine felt self-conscious as she rang the doorbell. Allie opened the door and gave Christine a big hug.

"You made it," she squealed. "I have missed you so much."

Christine winced. She felt guilty that she had ever questioned Allie's friendship. Seeing her again made it feel as if she had never left.

"Where's Brittany?" Christine asked.

"She had to go out. You know, haircut, facial, manicure. And then she's meeting Martin Drake for some pre-birthday celebrations," Allie said, rolling her eyes.

Christine looked at her friend blankly.

"Brittany and Martin can only occasionally make time for mere mortals like me. In fact, this is the first time I have seen her for weeks. And, as you can see, it's not exactly as though I'm spending quality time with her right now, is it?" Allie said ruefully.

Christine didn't know what to say. She was surprised that Brittany was so hot and heavy with Martin Drake. After all, he was Brittany's first serious boyfriend, and he was two years older than her. Christine was starting to wonder what else had changed in the time she had been gone.

Allie grabbed Christine's knapsack, and the girls headed up to one of the spare rooms. Allie raised her eyebrows slightly when she saw that Christine didn't have more luggage. Christine just shrugged, not wanting to tell her friend about deceiving her parents. It was better that Allie didn't know the details.

"I'm trying to travel light these days. Less hassle," Christine said, trying to sound nonchalant.

Allie gave Christine a quick update on her parents and her sister, and asked how Christine's mom and dad were doing. Christine's stomach twisted as she talked about how much her parents enjoyed life in Charlottetown.

"I can relate," Allie said, smiling. "They sound like my mom and dad. They can't wait to retire and get out of this city."

"I don't get it. Toronto is the place to be."

"Yeah, but what's PEI like?" Allie asked.

"It's better than I thought it would be," Christine admitted. "That doesn't mean that I'm going to stay."

"Why not?" Allie persisted.

"Everyone there has lived together for years. And I would never be an Islander," she struggled to explain.

Allie looked puzzled, but didn't ask any more.

"Let's go check out the mall," she said.

The girls went back downstairs and put on their jackets. There was an awkward silence as they walked in silence to the subway. Christine noticed that Allie's nose ring was gone and her friend was wearing jeans and a Gap sweatshirt.

"Brittany promises she'll meet us back here around six," Allie told Christine as they went through the turnstile and headed down the stairs to the subway platform. Christine felt strangely out of place in the crowd of people waiting for the train. She and Allie grabbed two seats on the subway and Christine blinked uncomfortably in the fluorescent light. Everyone on the train had the same blank expression and stared straight ahead.

The mall was crowded and noisy, and Christine didn't really see anything she liked. She bought a black sweater at The Gap for Brittany and then she and Allie went for lattes at their favourite coffee shop.

"Did you want the usual?" the salesgirl asked. Christine nodded, pleased that she had remembered her. She and her friends had spent many Saturday afternoons here over the last couple of years.

"Do you still see some of the old crowd from Bell?" Christine asked.

"The girls are so cliqueish and the guys are so full of themselves." Allie shrugged. "Everyone's still trying to fit in. The kids from Dieppe and Glenlawn are even bigger snobs than the kids we went to school with. And the school is gigantic."

Listening to Allie complain about North Park High, Christine decided that her friend was just trying to make her feel better because she wasn't there too. She looked at her watch, wondering what was happening in Charlottetown while she was sitting in a Toronto coffee shop. Finally, she excused herself and went to find a payphone to call her father. She nervously dialled her number at home and then punched in the number of the calling card that her parents had given her before they left Toronto. She was certain that this wasn't what they had in mind when they gave it to her. Never mind that now, she muttered to herself.

"Hi, Dad," Christine said, trying to sound upbeat. "How's it going on the legal front?"

"It turns out this is your lucky day. I called one of our company's lawyers, Gary Campbell. He's very interested in historical issues and he says he'll file that injunction on Monday," her father replied, his voice brimming with excitement. "What have you girls been doing all day? I was out around town and hoped to run into you to tell you the good news."

Christine's heart sank. "Uh, we were just putting up a few more posters and, um, calling people," she stammered.

"Do you girls want to come out for supper with us? My treat."

"Thanks, Dad, but we've got a ton of stuff to do before tomorrow," Christine lied, grimacing to herself.

"Oh, c'mon," her dad persisted. "Where are you calling from? It sounds busy."

"Just a coffee shop," Christine stuttered. "Downtown." She silently prayed that her father wouldn't ask her any more questions. She heard her mother saying something in the background.

"Your mother says somebody named Scott MacFarlane called," her dad said. "Do you want his number?"

Christine's stomach twisted in a knot at the mention of Scott's name. "No, I'm sure Jennifer knows it," she answered tensely. "He's just a guy from the lighthouse group." She hoped she didn't sound too defensive. Her father didn't seem to notice.

"Okay, don't stay up all night. You've got a big day ahead of you. We'll see you tomorrow."

Christine hung up and went back to the table where Allie was flipping through a magazine.

"Who were you calling?" Allie asked.

"Just checking my messages at home," Christine said nonchalantly, hoping that her friend wasn't going to get too nosy. After all, Allie had no idea that Christine was in Toronto without her parents' permission. That wouldn't be a big deal for Brittany, who was constantly doing things behind her parents' backs. But Christine knew that Allie would be shocked that Christine was sneaking around without her parents knowing where she was. It was better that she didn't know.

"So, what is there to do in Charlottetown?" Allie asked, finally closing the magazine and turning her attention to Christine.

"Well, I'm working on this great project for school," Christine said. "We're trying to save an old lighthouse."

Allie gave her a surprised look. "A lighthouse? Cool. Why does it need to be saved?"

"The Coast Guard wants to tear it down. We've got petitions and letters to the editor and we're going to have a protest tomorrow night," Christine explained. She went on to describe the lighthouse and the McIntoshes. Allie seemed interested in what Christine was saying, but Christine wondered if she was just being polite.

The girls grabbed the subway back to Brittany's house and were surprised to see a black BMW already in the driveway.

"That's Martin's car," Allie whispered, giving Christine a nudge.

Brittany came running to the door when Allie and Christine rang the bell. "You're here for my birthday, girl," Brittany shrieked, giving Christine a hug. Brittany was dressed all in black, with stylish boots. Her blonde hair was gelled into place and her makeup and nails were immaculate.

"Martin, Allie and Chrissie are here. My life is complete," Brittany yelled towards the kitchen. Martin Drake came striding out and gave the two girls a blank look.

"Martin, Chrissie. Chrissie, Martin," Brittany giggled. Martin gave Christine a bored look.

He was tall, with long, curly dark hair and wore baggy jeans and a Tommy Hilfiger sweatshirt. He was cute enough, Christine thought, but seemed a bit pouty now that he had to share Brittany with her friends.

"Isn't he a sweetie?" Brittany whispered.

"How's your birthday so far, Brittany?" Christine asked.

"It has been an excellent birthday," Brittany giggled, winking at Martin, who had slumped into a chair and was flipping through a copy of *Sports Illustrated*.

"Well, we've got to go get ready. We'll see you girls a bit later." Brittany walked over to Martin and grabbed his hand. They headed upstairs, leaving Christine and Allie standing in the entranceway.

Christine tried not to act surprised. She was hurt that her friend wasn't going to spend more time with her now. Oh well, Christine thought, I'll get a chance to talk to her later.

Chapter Sixteen

HAPPY BIRTHDAY, BRITTANY

By ten o'clock, Christine was miserable and ready to head back to Charlottetown. All night, Brittany was either hanging on Martin or whirling from room to room, accepting hugs and presents from a horde of well-wishers. Her parents were nowhere in sight but a series of maids went around the room carrying plates of hors d'oeuvres and platters full of pop in fancy crystal glasses. Christine imagined what her parents would think if they could see her now. They would be appalled at the sheer extravagance of the party.

"Are you having a good time, Chrissie?" Brittany gave her friend a squeeze as she swept past. She disappeared before Christine could answer.

Christine wished now that she had brought more clothes from Charlottetown. She was wearing her favourite black sweater and black pants, but almost all the girls at the party were in short skirts and tight-fitting sweaters. Christine noticed that they all wore lots of makeup. Even Allie was wearing makeup tonight, something she rarely did before Christine left.

Christine wondered where the Walkers were. Even Francesca was away. She was the one adult that Brittany occasionally listened to. Christine suspected that the housekeeper had no idea what her charge was up to for her birthday. Francesca loved Brittany dearly and did not go along with Brittany's wild plans.

Allie reappeared from the kitchen. She had gone to get some chips and pop for herself and Christine.

"The place is a total wreck." She grimaced.

"Francesca will have a few things to say about this," Christine nodded wryly, looking around the room at the destruction that the partying teenagers were causing. There were already a couple of smashed glasses, and food and dirty napkins everywhere.

"Who are all these people?" Allie asked. "This is the problem with North Park."

Christine tuned out her friend. Allie was getting on her nerves. All she wanted to do was complain about how bad her life was. Christine felt like telling her to shut up. After all, Christine was the one with the problem.

Feeling miserable, Christine thought about her conversation earlier in the day with her father. Why had Scott MacFarlane called? A cloud came over Christine's face. He knew that she was going to Toronto. Was he trying to get her in trouble? Oh well, she thought bitterly, it doesn't really matter. He would never be interested in someone from away.

"I'm going upstairs. I've had enough of this. You coming?" Allie asked.

Christine shook her head. "I want to talk to Brittany."

"Ha. Good luck," Allie said.

Christine felt like an idiot, sitting by herself in one of the sun rooms, sipping on Diet Coke and flipping through a magazine to keep awake.

Suddenly, she looked up and Martin was standing in the doorway.

"Oh, hi," he said, giving her a strange look. "You not having a good time?"

"No, I just thought I'd catch up on my reading," Christine replied, with a sarcastic grimace. She nervously took a sip of her Diet Coke. "It's warm," she said, choking slightly.

"Here, have some of this," Martin offered, sitting down on the couch and handed her a glass of ginger ale. Christine hesitated for a moment, not really wanting to drink from his glass. Martin gave her an encouraging nod. She took a sip and smiled thank you. She spluttered slightly and hoped Martin hadn't noticed. She wasn't sure what was in the glass but it definitely wasn't ginger ale. She felt a warm flush through her body.

"So, why haven't I seen you at North Park High?" Martin asked. Christine realized that he had no idea who she was or where she was living. She was angry that Brittany wouldn't have told him who she was.

"I live in Charlottetown now. I'm just back here for Brittany's birthday," Christine explained.

Martin took a minute to digest her explanation and swayed slightly. He handed her the glass again.

"No thanks," Christine said.

"C'mon, for Brittany." Martin playfully placed the glass on Christine's lips and tilted it back. She spluttered and the drink spilled all over her.

Martin didn't seem to notice. "Here's to Brittany," he toasted, his words slurring together. "So, why don't you go to North Park High?" he asked, again.

Christine was starting to feel sick to her stomach as the sip of Martin's drink mixed with the Diet Coke and potato chips.

Martin gave her a wobbly grin. "You know, you're kind of cute," he slurred. "Why haven't I met you before?"

Christine giggled. There was no sense trying to explain to him who she was or where she lived. She wondered what Brittany saw in this guy. He was obviously a jerk, and on top of that, he was clearly drunk.

Suddenly Martin Drake was leaning over her, pressing his body against hers. She felt his clammy lips against hers as he lowered her down onto the couch. Christine tried to push him away but he was too heavy. She started to panic and felt a wave of nausea from his breath and strong cologne.

Then, she heard Brittany's voice through a haze.

"I hate you," she was shouting.

Christine pushed Martin again and this time he moved. He got up from the couch, straightened his polo shirt and sauntered out of the room. Christine looked up into the face of a furious Brittany.

"What do you think you're doing?" she hissed at Christine.

"He kissed me," Christine stammered, trying to fix her shirt. She wiped her mouth with her hand, still feeling sick to her stomach. She looked at Brittany again and realized that her friend was totally misinterpreting the situation.

"I didn't mean he kissed me, kissed me. He just kissed me. I didn't want him to. Brittany, you've got to believe me," Christine faltered as she saw the fury on her friend's face.

"You've turned into a real slut all of a sudden," Brittany snapped, picking up Martin's glass and hurling it across the room. "You are so ungrateful. I give you a plane ticket and a place to live and what do you do? Throw yourself at my boyfriend."

"I did not. We were just talking and then he tried to kiss me."

"I doubt that," Brittany sneered. "Look at you. You are a mess. Your hair looks like crap and your clothes are totally out of date. Who could be bothered hitting on you?"

Christine realized that her friend was just angry but her words hurt. All evening, Christine had been feeling insecure among the richer, more stylish girls from Ontario.

"I didn't even want to be here in the first place," Christine said, her voice shaking. "I have friends and a new life on PEI. I was supposed to do something important this weekend but I came back here to see you. And you were too busy with him to even talk to me. I let my friends down and disappointed this old couple to be here this weekend."

It was all Christine could do to keep from bursting into tears.

Brittany's face turned pale and she turned and walked out of the room. Allie looked in from the doorway.

"Bad scene, I guess," Allie said quietly.

"What did you hear?" Christine sniffled.

"That Martin is bad news. I've tried to tell her. I'm sure he was hitting on you. Brittany just can't see it," Allie replied, sitting down on the couch.

"What am I going to do now?" Christine whimpered.

"Well, a good night's sleep would probably be a good idea. Do you know what time it is? I've been upstairs waiting for you two to finish partying." Allie giggled.

Christine started to giggle too as she realized that her friend was in her pajamas.

"Don't worry about Brittany," Allie added. "She'll calm down by the morning. We can spend the day together and everything will be fine."

"I have to get back to PEI," Christine said. "There's something I have to do. It's important."

"Is this the lighthouse thing?" Allie asked.

"Yeah." Christine was pleased that her friend remembered.

"What's happening tomorrow?"

Christine told Allie about the visit from the Minister of Heritage. Allie nodded encouragingly at Christine, who felt a sudden wave of homesickness for the lighthouse as she talked about the McIntoshes and their dilemma.

"Wow!" Allie said, enthusiastically as Christine finished her story. "That's really cool. I can't believe that you've done so much since you moved there."

"It's weird. I mean, I miss my life here but somehow I feel as though I really belong on PEI," Christine said softly.

"I'm sorry I haven't talked to you more," Allie replied, apologetically. "I've been so caught up in all my problems that I didn't even think about what you were going through. And I guess it has been kind of disappointing. For so long, we dreamed of going to North Park High and now, some days, I hate it. And I think, secretly, Brittany does too. She's used to being the most popular girl in school, and all of a sudden, the older girls hardly pay any attention to us."

"Why doesn't she talk about it?" Christine asked.

"I don't think Brittany will even admit there's anything wrong. The stuff with her parents is worse than ever. They fight all the time and they pay absolutely no attention to her. And this whole Martin Drake thing — he's such a bad influence on her." Allie shook her head.

Christine hoped she would say more but obviously Allie didn't want to give away their friend's secret.

"I guess we better hit the sack," Allie looked at her watch. "You've got a lighthouse to save after all."

"And I better save my friendship with Brittany before I go," Christine said. Allie gave her a quick hug and the girls headed upstairs to bed.

Chapter Seventeen

GOODBYE, AGAIN

*C*hristine awoke, not sure where she was. She looked over and saw Allie in the other bed across the room, still sleeping. Christine got up and looked out the window of the guest bedroom and gasped. The ground was covered in several feet of snow and a brisk wind was blowing drifts across the driveway.

Christine pulled on sweatpants and a sweatshirt and headed downstairs. She had to get to the airport as quickly as possible. When she walked into the kitchen, Brittany was sitting at the kitchen counter with a cup of coffee. Christine started to leave the room.

"Wait," Brittany said.

Christine stopped and turned to face her friend.

"I'm sorry, Brittany," Christine said quietly.

Brittany shook her head, frowning. "I really don't want to talk about it, Christine. Let's just forget it."

Christine knew that there was no point in trying to talk to Brittany when she was in a mood like this. She was sad that her friend looked so hurt. At the same time, it was like Brittany to turn this into a big melodrama.

"I guess we better get you to the airport," Brittany said finally.

"Right." Christine stammered. "I hope the snow won't make me late."

"It started around three o'clock, just as the party was breaking up," Brittany explained. "Not that I remember much of it," Brittany added, wincing as she picked up a cold cloth from the table and put it across her forehead.

Christine wondered why her friend was behaving so strangely. She couldn't believe that Brittany had been drinking last night. She had never done anything like that before. Christine held back a shudder as she recalled Martin's hot alcohol-laced breath pressing against her face.

Brittany tilted her head back slightly and put her feet up on a chair.

"Grab some coffee," she suggested to Christine, pointing to a pot on the counter.

Christine poured herself a cup of coffee and sat down at the kitchen table.

Brittany gave her a direct look and smiled sheepishly. "I'm sorry you didn't have a better time at the party."

"Brittany, it wasn't what you think," Christine protested.

Brittany put her hands up in the air. "Chrissie, I don't want to get into it. I was wrong. He's a jerk, okay?"

Christine wasn't satisfied but she didn't know what else to say to her friend. Brittany was often like this — mad one minute, friendly the next. Allie said that Brittany learned this from her parents, who were always fighting. Usually one of them ended up storming out of the house and going somewhere else to stay. Then the other parent acted as if nothing had happened. No wonder Brittany was so screwed up.

Today, though, she had other things on her mind. She had to get back to the Island. She glanced at her watch. It was already eleven o'clock in Charlottetown.

"I've got to phone the airline," she said, looking apologetically at Brittany. "There's something I've got to do back home."

Christine quickly called the airline at the number listed on her ticket.

"I'm sorry, miss, but all our flights are on hold right now until the weather clears up," the ticket agent said.

"When will the next flight be leaving for Halifax?" Christine asked, shaking with desperation.

"I'd advise you to come down to the airport and be ready to fly stand-by," the agent replied. "I'm afraid that's the best we can do."

Christine hung up and told Brittany what had happened.

"Let's call a limo, quick, and get you to the airport." Brittany smiled. Allie had joined her in the kitchen. She glanced from one friend to the other. Christine gave her a slight nod and Allie smiled, recognizing that the two girls were talking again.

Christine looked over at her two friends. Their hair was a mess and they hadn't had time to put on any makeup. Sitting there in their pajamas, the three of them looked the way they had when they were younger, when they used to have slumber parties.

"I've screwed everything up," Christine said, thinking of Mack and Betty.

"I'm sorry that I was such an idiot," Brittany answered. "I mean, you came all this way for my party and I didn't get to talk to you all night."

Christine winced slightly, but Brittany grabbed her in a big hug. "I guess we've all gone through a lot of changes," Brittany said, with a wistful smile.

"But we miss you, Chrissie," Allie piped in.

"I miss you too, but I guess my family is in Charlottetown to stay so I'd better get used to it," Christine answered.

"And I'm dumping that Martin Drake," Brittany declared. "I don't know what I saw in him in the first place. I was just trying to fit in," she concluded. The girls were silent for a moment.

"Hey, shouldn't we get this girl to the airport? Look out, Island, here she comes!" Allie shouted, and the three friends rushed upstairs to get dressed.

As the airport limousine weaved its way through the familiar streets of Toronto, the girls talked about the party. It was like old times.

"Did you tell Brittany about your meeting tonight?" Allie asked. Christine shook her head.

"Tell her. It's so cool!" Allie urged.

As the limo headed onto the 401 and picked up speed, Christine and Allie filled Brittany in about the plan to save the lighthouse. Christine listened with pleasure as Allie described all the work that Christine was doing to save the lighthouse.

Christine did some quick math in her head. "I can't make it back in time for the protest," she told her friends. "But I can still make it for the questions after the Minister's speech. I really want to be there."

She blushed slightly when she told them about Scott, and the girls nudged her in a teasing way.

"I don't have a chance with him," Christine said, shaking her head. "He's mad because I came here instead of staying to save the lighthouse. And besides, I'm from away."

"You're what?" Allie giggled. "It sounds like some kind of disease."

"It might as well be," Christine replied sarcastically. She explained about Jennifer's friends and how they looked down on her because she wasn't an Islander.

"I think they're just jealous," Brittany suggested. "I'm sure they feel threatened because you come from the big city and have all kinds of stuff that they don't. But I think you should give this Scott guy a chance. Maybe he'll figure out that girls from away aren't so bad after all."

Christine looked over at her friend fondly. "I just hope he'll give me a chance," she said wistfully. "I guess the first thing is to save the lighthouse. Then maybe he'll talk to me again."

"You know, you really do seem to like it there, after all," Allie observed, watching Christine's face light up as she told them about Betty and Dave McIntosh.

"We're happy for you," Brittany added. "And you know what, North Park High is not such a hot place, after all. We're the youngest ones there, and, well, I kind of miss the way things used to be."

When they arrived at the airport, the girls rushed to the Air Canada ticket counter. The computer screens were lit up with flights that had been cancelled or postponed.

"Oh great," Christine sighed.

The next flight to Halifax was leaving in half an hour. The agent quickly checked the computer to see if there was space.

"If they get the runways cleared, we may be able to get out in time to catch the last connecting flight to Charlottetown. Otherwise you'll have to overnight in Halifax," the agent said.

"I have to get home," Christine muttered under her breath, trying to smile sweetly at the same time.

At the security gate, she and Brittany looked at each other awkwardly. Then Brittany grabbed Christine and gave her a quick hug.

"I'm sorry about everything," Brittany whispered as Christine picked up her knapsack.

"I'm glad I came," Christine replied, honestly. Brittany ran off to use the phone, leaving Allie and Christine to say goodbye.

"She's not going to phone him, is she?" Christine asked, raising her eyebrows at Allie.

Her friend shrugged. "With Brittany, anything is possible. At least the two of you seem to be getting along okay now."

"I don't understand how she could be so mad at me last night, and today it's completely forgotten," Christine shook her head.

"That's just Brittany. She couldn't stand it if she felt you were mad at her. She needs everyone to like her," Allie theorized.

"Even Martin Drake?" Christine wondered, almost to herself.

"I'll believe she's breaking up with him when I see it. Brittany isn't always great at doing something that may mean someone won't like her," Allie replied.

The girls paused for a moment and listened to the boarding announcement for Christine's flight.

"Time to go," Allie gave Christine another hug. "Good luck. I'm sure you'll make it for your meeting."

Brittany came running up just as Christine was about to leave.

"I just checked my messages. I forgot to check them last night," Brittany paused to catch her breath. "Someone must have been on the phone when they called."

"When who called?" Christine asked urgently.

"Your parents," Brittany said. "They sounded worried. Your mom wanted you to call her right away. What's wrong?"

"What?" Christine moaned. "Oh no. They're going to kill me."

"Why?" Allie asked, puzzled.

Christine looked at her friends. She had forgotten that they didn't know that she was there without her parents' permission. "It's a long story." Christine sighed. "I've got to go."

Her stomach was churning as she ran the length of the terminal to her gate. Once she took her seat, she realized she was shaking. She was beyond feeling miserable, almost numb. She pushed all thoughts of her parents out of her mind and tried to concentrate on willing the plane to take off.

"I'm afraid we're going to have a short delay this afternoon," the flight attendant said over the speaker system. "They are going to have to de-ice our wings before take-off, and because of all the delays, we are fifth in line. We should be taking off in about twenty minutes."

Christine sighed in frustration. She was desperate to get back to the Island and set things right. She knew that her parents were going to be furious and she couldn't really blame them. This time, she had gone too far.

Looking back, she wasn't sure why she had been so determined to come back to Toronto. Her life here seemed so long ago now. She had moved on and so, to some degree, had Brittany and Allie. She felt as if she was leaving them of her own accord this time. It was her choice.

Her parents, however, would never understand. She had betrayed their trust in the worst possible way, and she knew she was in deep trouble.

After another fifteen minutes passed, Christine's numbness turned to panic. She glanced at her watch. Time was ticking away and she was still no closer to Charlottetown. She closed her eyes and leaned back against the seat. The full impact of the weekend hit her suddenly and she felt a wave of nausea. How had she been so stupid? She had lied to her parents, disappointed the McIntoshes who had been so kind to her and almost lost her two best friends in the bargain. She vowed to learn a lesson from the weekend.

Allie was right, Christine thought to herself. I think I will like living in Charlottetown, if I give it a fair chance. She only hoped her parents were going to give her another chance.

She felt the plane's engines surging as the aircraft finally pulled onto the runway. She gripped the sides of her seat and sank back into her chair as the plane took off, winging towards the East Coast.

The time seemed to drag. She kept checking her watch, praying that she would get to Halifax in time to catch the connecting flight to Halifax. As they were preparing to land in Halifax, she gazed out the window in terror. It was already dark.

"Oh my gosh," she mumbled to herself. "It's already seven-thirty."

The next plane to Charlottetown left Halifax at eight o'clock. It was a twenty-five minute flight, then another fifteen minutes downtown. Christine would just make it in time for the end of the meeting.

"Please let me get there in time to show them that I do care what happens," she pleaded silently. "And please, please let my parents forgive me."

Chapter Eighteen

THE HERITAGE MINISTER

As soon as her flight from Toronto landed, Christine pushed her way to the front of the plane and dashed down towards the end of the terminal where the flights for the Island boarded. She handed her boarding pass breathlessly to the agent.

"You're going to have to take a seat, miss," the agent said politely. "We're waiting for a connecting flight from Ottawa."

"But I've got to get to Charlottetown for a meeting," she gasped.

"The snowstorm has wrecked everyone's travel plans," the agent said sympathetically. "The Heritage Minister was supposed to be in Charlottetown for some big speech and she is still just on her way here from Ottawa. We've been asked to hold the flight for her."

It took a minute for her words to sink in. Christine went over to one of the couches and sank into a seat. Had she heard that right? The Heritage Minister had been snowed in too and was going to be on her flight? That meant she wasn't going to miss the meeting after all. She felt a wave of relief. Then she remembered all the people waiting to meet the Minister in Charlottetown and her heart sank. They were going to be disappointed. And what would happen to the McIntoshes now?

Christine looked up and saw an elegantly attired woman with grey hair swept up in a bun being hurried along by a younger woman with glasses and a big briefcase. Christine recognized Jane Thompson from the news. The Heritage Minister had made the flight.

Christine's heart was pounding as she climbed the steps to the tiny plane that would take them across the Northumberland Strait to Charlottetown. It was the same flight that she had taken yesterday morning but that seemed like weeks ago. So much had happened.

Christine was seated two rows back from the Heritage Minister. As she walked past, Jane Thompson was already skimming through a thick binder. The worried-looking young woman, who was seated on the aisle, flipped through her briefcase pulling out a wad of papers. The Minister looked up as Christine walked by and smiled.

Once the plane was in the air, Christine summoned up all her courage and made her way up the aisle to the Minister's row.

"Excuse me," she said in her most polite voice.

Jane Thompson looked up, surprised.

"I don't mean to bother you, but I was wondering if I could just speak with you for a moment," Christine asked firmly, gripping her hands together so they wouldn't shake.

"I'm afraid the Minister is really busy," the young executive assistant piped in, getting up and blocking Christine's view of the Minister. "We have to prepare for a meeting in Charlottetown and we're running behind schedule."

Christine stood speechless, as the assistant sat back down. Her knees were shaking as she slowly walked back to her seat. As she slumped by the window, Christine stared out at the lakes and forests of Nova Scotia. They were almost at the shore. In minutes, they would be over the Strait, heading directly towards the Governors Light.

Christine was devastated. She pictured the McIntoshes sitting in their cozy parlour, sipping their tea, as the plane carrying the Minister floated high above them. Christine felt like a failure. She had let everyone down, and she knew that things were only going to get worse when she arrived back on the Island.

"May I sit down for a moment?" a voice inquired and Christine jolted up in her seat. She looked up to see Jane Thompson smiling in her direction.

"Uh, sure," Christine stammered.

"I have to apologize for my assistant's rudeness," the Minister said in a hushed voice. "She means well and we are behind schedule. But I always have time for a young Canadian who needs to speak to me." Jane Thompson settled into the seat beside Christine. "Now, what can I do for you?"

"It's about the Governors Light," Christine began, gripping the arms of her seat nervously. She was tired, but she felt a surge of adrenaline, the way she felt towards the end of a 10k race. Focus, Christine, focus, she thought to herself.

"Ah yes, the old lighthouse," the Heritage Minister nodded. "The Coast Guard wants to tear it down, don't they?"

"That's the problem," Christine continued, gathering strength. "An old couple lives there and they have ever since they got married. He was the lightkeeper and they promised he could stay. He has lived in lighthouses all his life."

The Minister nodded sympathetically. "It's a matter of finances, though, I'm afraid." Jane Thompson sighed. "I would save all of them if I could. But my Cabinet colleagues don't always agree with me."

"We have a plan," Christine explained, encouraged by the Minister's supportive response. "Some of the local builders say they can salvage the lighthouse. They would need some money for materials but we think we can raise enough in sponsorships and from fund-raisers," Christine continued. "All we need from you is a commitment to designate the lighthouse a historic site. And it is historic. My mom has been doing some research. It is a unique lighthouse in Atlantic Canada."

Christine smiled as she thought of Mack's storage shed, filled with artifacts from the old lights. She told the Minister about the lightkeeper's incredible collection — the old photographs, the brass bell from an ancient schooner, the tattered ropes and rusty anchors and all the other pieces of Island maritime history. Christine smiled as she described the beauty of the giant glass light itself.

The Minister was silent for a moment. Christine held her breath. She looked out the window and saw the Governors Light ahead in the distance.

"There it is," Christine exclaimed, pointing out the window.

The Heritage Minister leaned over and gazed out.

"It is beautiful," she said softly and they both stared at the light flickering in the darkness as the plane started its descent over the Charlottetown harbour.

The flight attendant announced that they were preparing to land and Jane Thompson got up to return to her seat.

"What is your name?" she said, turning to Christine as she got up.

"Christine Miller," Christine replied.

The Heritage Minister reached out her hand to Christine. "You've made a compelling argument," Jane Thompson said. "I will see what I can do. But I can't promise anything," she added as she disappeared back to her seat.

Chapter Nineteen

SAVE OUR LIGHTHOUSE!

Christine closed her eyes. She was exhausted by the events of the weekend. Still, a smile drifted across her face as she thought about what the Heritage Minister had said. Jane Thompson had made no promises but Christine felt that she had done her best.

The Heritage Minister was hurried off the plane by her assistant. Christine grabbed her knapsack and made her way down the steps of the small plane and headed to the terminal. As she walked towards the sliding doors, she saw the silhouettes of people carrying signs. Oh no, she whispered to herself, they're protesting at the airport. She felt suddenly embarrassed at the thought of the kids from her school seeing her get off the plane.

Christine realized she had no choice but to go in through the doors. She tried to sneak around the side of the group of protesters. She recognized several kids from her school and thought she saw Jennifer's dad. They were chanting, "Save our lighthouse," and waving signs in the Minister's direction. A television camera with a light on pointed towards the small but vocal group, and a reporter was standing talking to the Minister near the baggage carousel.

Christine was almost out the door when she heard someone call her name. She turned to see her parents standing on the edge of the crowd. Her mother rushed over to her and grabbed her in a big hug.

"Christine, what were you thinking?" her mother whispered in her ear, hugging her even tighter.

"We have a lot of talking to do," her father said sternly.

"I'm so sorry," Christine said, her eyes welling up with tears, still clinging to her mother. "I'm sorry about everything. I should never have lied to you."

"We're just happy you're back safe and sound," her mother answered, looking pleadingly in her husband's direction.

Christine's dad still looked fierce. "We'll talk more later," he said, in an ominous voice.

Just then, the crowd grew quiet as the Minister approached the group of protesters.

"I'm sorry that I was not able to attend the meeting at the Confederation Centre tonight," the Minister said, addressing the crowd. The television camera rushed around to record her words. Christine noticed Jennifer and Scott at the front of the crowd of protesters. Jennifer glanced over in Christine's direction. She appeared surprised when she saw Christine standing with her parents.

"I have heard the concerns you have about your lighthouse," Jane Thompson continued. "I had an interesting conversation on the airplane with a member of your group, Christine Miller," she added. "It was most informative and I agree that the situation needs further study before any action is taken."

The crowd cheered.

"I'm not making any commitments," she cautioned. "But I will have my department look into it."

The protesters burst into applause. Christine turned to her parents and smiled but her mother still looked anxious and her father frowned. Christine felt the smile melt from her face.

She gazed over at the crowd and saw Dave and Betty McIntosh posing for a picture with the Heritage Minister. Jane Thompson was having an animated conversation with Mack. Christine wondered what stories he was telling her about the lighthouse, his pride and joy. She looked over where Jennifer and Scott were standing. Jennifer's eyes met hers, and then the other girl deliberately turned away.

As the Heritage Minister and her assistant were whisked past, out to a waiting limo, the Minister forced the group to stop.

"Nice meeting you, Christine," Jane Thompson said, shaking Christine's hand again. Christine quickly introduced her parents.

"We'll be in touch," the Minister added, as she rushed out the door.

The protest group was breaking up now and heading for their cars. Christine caught a glimpse of Betty and Dave McIntosh, standing by the baggage carousel with Jennifer's father.

"I'll be right back," she said to her parents.

She walked over to the McIntoshes. Mack was leaning heavily on Betty, and seemed tired after his conversation with the Minister.

"We heard you had left us for Toronto," Mack said. "But I knew, my girl, that you wouldn't let us down." Christine was sad to hear that the old couple had heard about her trip to Ontario. She had hoped that they would never even know that she was gone. Now she felt as if she had betrayed them.

"You've done a good deed for us," Betty added.

Christine shook her head. "It's not a sure thing yet," she said quietly. "And I'm sorry that I almost did let you down. If the Minister hadn't been on that plane ..."

"Aye, but she was," Mack replied sternly. "You've got the luck of an Islander, my girl. You were meant to live by the sea."

Christine felt a wave of fatigue come over her as she and the McIntoshes walked out into the dark night. Her parents were silent as Christine said farewell to the McIntoshes and got into the Jeep. It was a tense and quiet ride to their house. Christine went up to her room without saying a word. She knew that the wrath of her parents was still to come. She wished they could feel some pride in what she had accomplished for the lighthouse. She had ruined that, she thought ruefully.

Chapter Twenty

THE ULTIMATUM

Christine felt very conspicuous at school Monday. As she walked through the hallways, the other students whispered and pointed. She was surprised when some smiled encouragingly in her direction.

"Why are they looking at me?" she asked Jennifer, as they took their seats in Social Studies class. "They can't all know about my trip to Ontario."

"Haven't you seen the cover of *The Guardian*? It's you shaking hands with the Minister," Jennifer said with a sneer.

Christine groaned. "Great, that's all I need."

"What? I thought you'd be happy. Don't you people from Ontario love to be centre stage?" Jennifer replied. Christine had never heard Jennifer use this tone of voice before. She knew that her friend was mad, but she hadn't expected her to be mean.

"My parents are furious with me," Christine explained. "My dad wants to have a talk tonight. This is just going to add fuel to his fire."

Jennifer turned away, not bothering to reply.

"Why are you so mad at me?" Christine asked.

Jennifer raised her eyebrows. "I don't understand why you had to go. But how could I? I've lived in the same place all my life. What do I know? I'm just another stupid Islander."

"Jennifer, I never thought you were stupid. That's not fair," Christine snapped back.

"Well, it took someone from Ontario to save our lighthouse, didn't it?" Jennifer replied. Christine wanted to continue the argument but their teacher was calling the class to order.

Ms. Carpenter started class by holding up the cover of *The Guardian*. "A couple of your classmates have taken this Social Studies project to heart." The teacher grinned. "Christine, can you and Jennifer give us an update on the Governors Lighthouse project?"

Jennifer glared at Christine, and reluctantly they got up in front of the class. Jennifer gave them a quick synopsis of the protest they had planned — and how their plans had to be changed at the last minute when the Minister's plane was delayed because of the snowstorm.

"That's where Christine came in," Jennifer said, in a cold voice.

Christine described her conversation with the Minister. "I asked her to designate the lighthouse a national historic site," Christine explained. "That way, the Coast Guard can't tear it down. It was my mom's idea, actually. She's been helping us with our research."

"The Coast Guard has set a deadline of the end of this month," Jennifer interjected. "So it's critical that we get an answer from the Minister on the heritage status as soon as possible."

"A lawyer has filed an injunction on behalf of the McIntoshes to prevent the demolition, at least until the heritage status is determined," Christine continued. She was surprised that Jennifer knew about the letter from the Coast Guard. Then she realized that Jennifer must have been talking to the McIntoshes over the weekend.

"What are the chances of having the lighthouse named a heritage site?" Ms. Carpenter inquired.

"We're not sure," Christine replied. "Our research shows that the lighthouse is unique in many ways. And so many of them have been torn down. But it's really up to the Minister."

"Well, let us know if you hear anything," their teacher asked, as the girls took their seats. The class burst into applause, making them blush. But Jennifer still refused to look in Christine's direction.

Christine and Jennifer were mobbed by their classmates after the bell rang. Jennifer broke away from the crowd and headed in the opposite direction. Christine thought about chasing after her, but decided against it. She wasn't sure what she could say that would change her friend's mind about her trip to Ontario. The damage was done.

Christine was already tense over her fight with Jennifer when she arrived home. Her mother was waiting for her, and she wasn't smiling.

"Your father called to say that he was going to be late. But he wants to talk to you as soon as he gets home," Monica said, as Christine carried her knapsack upstairs to her room. She looked at the pile of posters on her desk, and felt a fresh wave of embarrassment over what she had done. Christine sighed. What a mess she had made of everything!

When she came down to the kitchen, her mother was starting supper. She handed the peeler over to Christine and pointed to a stack of potatoes.

"Are you mad at me too?" Christine asked quietly.

Her mother paused. "I'm not mad, Chrissie, as much as disappointed. I thought that you truly were making an effort to fit in here. Obviously I was wrong."

"It's not that I don't like it here," Christine corrected her. "I just needed to really find out where I belonged — here or back in Toronto."

"That doesn't mean you should sneak away behind our backs," her mother rebuked her. "I was so embarrassed, and Jennifer was embarrassed too. What kind of a friend are you to ask her to lie?"

Monica paused and looked into her daughter's face. "How does that make us look when you can jet off to Toronto and we don't know? We're not like Brittany's parents. We do like to have some idea of where you are and what you're doing."

"Brittany and Allie aren't as bad as you think," Christine replied defensively. "They don't really like North Park very much. And when you get them away from the country club, and all the snobs there, they're really just ordinary girls."

Monica gave her daughter a weak smile. "You are a good friend, Christine, and I'm sorry if this has been hard on you. But you have gone too far this time. It's one thing to be unhappy about moving. It's another thing to go to Toronto behind our backs."

"Can you please put in a good word for me with Dad?" Christine pleaded.

"I think you and your dad have some things to work out," Monica replied. "You know, he feels he is to blame. He thought that he made your life miserable by forcing you to move. Then when you seemed to like it here and got involved with the lighthouse, he was so relieved. But he was hurt all over again when he found out you had gone to Toronto."

Christine and her mother continued to prepare supper, but there was none of the usual chatter. Christine was cleaning the family room when her dad arrived home around six o'clock.

"Let's have supper before you talk," Monica suggested.

"No, let's get this over with," Christine pleaded. Her father looked slightly surprised. He motioned for her to follow him into the family room. Monica sighed and returned to the kitchen.

"I'm sorry, Dad," Christine burst into her explanation before her father even had a chance to sit down. "I was an idiot to go to Toronto and especially not to tell you and Mom. I didn't do it to bother you. I just didn't know what to do. I wanted to see Brittany and Allie and I wanted to be here. So, I tried to do both."

Her father listened silently. Then he took a wad of papers from his briefcase and threw them down on the table beside Christine. "Here's your injunction," he said testily.

Christine caught her breath. While her father was calling in favours to help her save the lighthouse, she had been off gallivanting in Toronto behind his back.

"I didn't mean to lie to you ..." Christine began, desperate to set things right. But her father waved his arms in the air.

"Whoa, Chrissie," he ordered tersely. "Enough, enough. It's not me that you let down with your shenanigans. It was the McIntoshes. I thought that you had learned your lesson, that you were starting to think about someone besides yourself. But obviously I was wrong.

"I went out to the lighthouse to get them to sign the injunction, and you know what — Jennifer was there and you weren't. I asked her where you were and to her credit, she defended you as best she could," Rob's eyes smoldered with anger. Christine was horrified, and speechless.

"The look on the faces of those lovely, old people when they found out you had gone to Toronto on the very weekend when they needed you most ... I was embarrassed, for you and for myself as your father."

"I'm so sorry," she said.

"I think there's only one thing for you to do now," her father continued, the tension etched in his face. "You have to quit the campaign to save the lighthouse."

Christine's eyes grew wide with horror. "I can't quit!" she sputtered. "That's the worst thing you could ask me to do."

"I think it's only fair," her father replied adamantly. "You can't be trusted. I don't want you letting that old couple down again. This is one way to guarantee it."

Christine was furious. She ran out of the room, tears streaming down her face. Grabbing her windbreaker, she rushed out of the door.

"Chrissie, come back," her mother cried.

But Christine was already on her way down the street, racing towards the boardwalk.

Chapter Twenty-One

APOLOGIES

Christine walked up and down the boardwalk, still shaking from the confrontation with her dad. She desperately needed to talk to the McIntoshes. That was the only way she could resolve this problem with her father.

The wind was starting to pick up and blew in hard off the frozen water on the harbour. Christine shivered in her light windbreaker. She started to run to keep warm. The steady rhythm of her feet on the boardwalk kept time with the flashing pulse of the light. Christine was heartened to see the now-familiar flash of light in the increasing darkness. It strengthened her determination to continue to fight to save the lighthouse.

Christine was startled as a car drove by and honked. She started to run even faster, turning her face away from the road that ran alongside the boardwalk.

"Christine!" a familiar voice shouted. Christine breathed a sigh of relief as she turned towards the road. It was Scott MacFarlane, in a car driven by someone else.

"Where are you going in such a hurry?" He grinned. "Track practice?"

Any other time, Christine would have been thrilled to joke around with Scott. But tonight she had other things on her mind.

"Could you drive me out to the lighthouse?" she asked desperately.

"Just a second," he shouted back. He turned and consulted the car's driver. Scott seemed to be explaining something to the driver, who eventually nodded. "Hop in," Scott called to her, twisting around to open the back door. Christine climbed into the car, a battered old VW Rabbit.

"This is my brother Doug," Scott said, turning to face Christine. She gave Doug a half-hearted wave. Doug was a few years older than Scott. He was also good-looking in a rugged, outdoorsy kind of way.

"Why the rush to go out to the light?" Scott asked, as Doug steered the car along North River Road, heading out to the Trans-Canada Highway. Christine paused for a moment, turning to look down her street to see if her parents were looking for her. There was no sign of anyone outside her house, and both family vehicles were still in the driveway.

"It's my dad," Christine said, trying to make her voice sound calm. Running along the boardwalk had helped clear her mind, but suddenly being in close proximity with Scott had jumbled her thoughts again. "He wants me to quit the lighthouse project."

Scott gave a low whistle. "Wow, that's tough," he said sympathetically. "Why does he want you to quit?"

"Because I took off to Toronto to go to my friend's birthday and I didn't tell my parents. I let everyone down." The words came tumbling out. Christine told Scott the whole story, omitting a few details like the incident with Martin Drake. When she was finished, she sat in dejected silence. She was certain that Scott would think she was a total jerk now, if he didn't already.

Scott gestured to his brother to turn off the highway into the parking lot of the Tim Hortons. He reached into his jeans and handed Christine a quarter. She looked at him with shock. Was he kicking her out of the car?

"Go phone your parents," Scott said. "You don't want things to get any worse than they already are. Then we'll go on to the lighthouse."

Christine paused for a minute, staring at Scott. He gave her a reassuring nod and pointed to the phone. She looked to see if Doug was laughing. But the older MacFarlane sat stoically in the front seat, fiddling with the radio dial. Christine ran to the phone booth and dialled. Her mother answered the phone on the first ring.

"Chrissie, what's going on? Your father is pacing around here like a caged lion."

"I need to talk to Dad," Christine said quietly. "Everything will be okay, Mom."

She heard her mother pass the phone over to her father. "Where are you?" he said sternly, though she could hear the concern in his voice.

"I'm on my way to talk to the McIntoshes," Christine explained. "I need to make things right. And then, if you insist, I'll quit the lighthouse group."

Her father sighed. "Chrissie, just come home. We'll talk this thing through."

"No, this is something I have to do," she replied stubbornly. "Scott MacFarlane and his brother are giving me a ride out. Scott's a guy from school who's part of the lighthouse group. I'll be home as soon as I can."

"Are you sure this is what you want to do?"

"Yes, I am."

"We'll talk more when you get home then. Don't be too late. Your mother will worry."

When she got back to the car, Scott and Doug were waiting. "Is everything okay at home?" Scott asked. Christine nodded. Doug started the car and headed towards the road that would take them to the lighthouse.

The stars were beginning to appear overhead as the Rabbit made its way down the highway. After about five minutes of silence, Christine gathered up her courage.

"I guess you think I'm just a spoiled brat from away," she said, so quietly it was almost a whisper. Scott turned to her in surprise.

"No, the exact opposite, in fact," he answered. "I'll admit I was a little confused when you went back to Toronto the weekend of the protest. But then I put myself in your shoes. I asked myself what it would be like to move someplace and leave everyone you cared about behind. And besides you had the guts to go up and talk to the Minister. I'm not sure I would have done that."

"Oh, you've got quite the mouth on you, Scotty. I'm sure you would have done the same," Doug piped up and all three teenagers burst into laughter.

As they drove up to the lighthouse, Scott stared up out of the window.

"She's a beauty," he murmured.

Christine jumped out of the back seat, eager to get to the lighthouse and see the McIntoshes. She paused halfway to the door and turned around. Scott and Doug hadn't moved.

"You're coming too, aren't you?" Christine pleaded, looking from one MacFarlane to the other.

"I'll wait in the car," Doug said firmly.

"Are you sure?" Scott asked Christine.

"Yes, you've already set me right once tonight," she said, smiling shyly in his direction as they walked together to the steps leading to the door of the lighthouse. "I could use the moral support."

Christine knocked firmly on the door. Betty peeked out of the window to see who it was. Christine gave her a friendly wave.

"Why, Christine ... and Scott. What a nice surprise," Betty gave them a kind smile as she ushered them through the door. She looked slightly puzzled at the two teenagers. "Were we expecting you?"

"No, this is a special visit," Christine replied, somewhat taken aback that Mrs. McIntosh knew Scott.

"And how are your folks?" Betty asked Scott. Before he could answer, she explained to Christine, "Scott's people have fished for years. And his father was a friend of our son's. Before he left for away," she added wistfully. She gestured for the two young people to have a seat.

Mack came into the sitting room, with the Old Salt close behind, followed by Marco Polo, who was wagging his tail as he came over to greet the visitors.

"What is this now? To what do we owe the pleasure of this fair visit?" Mack said, giving their hands a hearty shake, though Christine noticed that his hands were trembling slightly. The Old Salt settled into the rocking chair by the fire.

"I needed to talk to you and Betty," Christine said, feeling suddenly awkward, especially with the Old Salt staring at her curiously. "I need to, uh, apologize."

"Apologize for what, my dear?" Betty piped in.

"For letting you down. By going to Toronto. I, uh, I'm so sorry," Christine murmured softly.

"No need to apologize," Mack bellowed, giving a hearty grin in Christine's direction. "You're a gal with some gumption, that's all I can say." And he and Old Salt guffawed loudly.

"But my dad says I have to quit the lighthouse project now," Christine continued, slightly bewildered by their jovial response.

That silenced the old lightkeeper. "You don't need to quit on our account," he replied seriously. "You have to do what you want to do."

"I want to save this place. I ... love it," Christine blurted.

"I'm sure your father will understand that," Betty said kindly. Christine nodded sadly. She sensed that her father was serious about his intention to have her quit the lighthouse project, but when she looked around the room at the McIntoshes, and Old Salt, she was filled with a feeling of warmth. Slowly, she felt the worries of the last couple of days melting away.

"I've got just the thing to liven things up," blustered the Old Salt, never one to leave the room quiet for long. He pulled out a guitar from a case beside the rocking chair. Marco Polo watched every movement his owner made and seemed to perk up when he saw the guitar. Scott and Christine exchanged looks, and Christine found herself blushing as she looked away.

"I've got a tune about the wreck of the SAVINTA in 19 and 6," the Old Salt explained, as he strummed his guitar. He broke into song, his gravelly voice the perfect accompaniment for the melancholy story he was about to tell.

Come all you jolly seamen bold
and listen unto me.
Twas the loss of the ship SAVINTA
in November blustery.

Twas on the fourth of November
when she first did set sail.
And scarcely had she laid her course
When she encountered with a gale.

Until the sixth that dreadful night
A storm there did arise
The raging billows loud did roar

And dismal were the skies.

They battled with the heavy seas
Those sailors young and brave.
For well they thought, their time had come
To meet a watery grave.

Two Island boys stood upon the sand
Their grieving hearts were sore.
They looked around for a boat secure
To bring the sailors to shore.

There was a dory on the beach
But she was small and frail.
They quickly launched her in the sea
To face the raging gale.

But there she filled and filled again.
Amid the deafening roar.
They tried again and yet again
And at last they came to the shore.

But ten poor souls had lost their lives
They were noble, young and brave.
So pray now for your comrades lost
Who met a watery grave.

Christine was amazed to feel tears welling up in her eyes as the Old Salt finished his song. She looked at the two old men. Both were filled with stories and memories of the sea, of its beauty and at the same time its cruelty.

"We'd better get going," Scott said, softly, snapping Christine back to reality.

"Come again soon, dear," Betty whispered, giving Christine a hug.

"And if that father of yours gives you any more trouble, you tell him he'll have to answer to me," Mack shouted as Christine followed Scott out the door. She gave the couple a cheerful wave.

Doug was crouched by the shore, staring out across the water. He joined them at the car.

"Thanks for waiting," Christine said gratefully. Doug nodded. They drove back in silence to Charlottetown, all three lost in their own thoughts about the visit to the old lighthouse. In the back seat, Christine looked from one brother to the other, wondering what they were thinking about. She had heard that Scott's father fished for lobster, and she had overheard Scott telling Betty that Doug was hoping to take over the boat as soon as he was finished school. She wondered if Scott wanted to become a fisherman like his father and brother. Again, she was struck by how much more mature her Island friends were than Allie and Brittany. Life was tougher here in many ways, she thought sadly, thinking again of the young men from the song.

When they arrived at Christine's house, she thanked Doug, who gave her a nonchalant wave from the front seat. Scott got out of the car and walked her up the front steps. They stood for a moment, awkwardly, on the porch. Suddenly, Christine remembered Scott's phone call while she was in Toronto.

"I'm sorry I didn't call you back," Christine said, her voice shaking slightly. Then she blushed.

Scott turned to her and, to her surprise, he too was blushing. "Actually I was just looking for an excuse to call you," he replied, sheepishly. "I was hoping I could convince you to talk to the Heritage Minister with me. I thought maybe you had decided not to go to Toronto after all."

Christine's smiled faded as she realized that she had disappointed Scott as well as everyone else. "I'm sorry," she whispered, sitting back against the porch railing.

"I told you, I understand," Scott replied. "And it all worked out in the end, right?"

Christine looked into the lit hallway, where her parents were waiting for her. She hoped that didn't mean another fight with her father. "Thanks again," she said. "I really needed to talk to the McIntoshes tonight. You've been a big help." She hoped that didn't sound too idiotic.

"I hope it goes well with your dad." Scott's voice was sincere. He looked for a second as if he wanted to say something else. Then, he seemed to think better of it and gave her a quick wave. He jumped down the stairs and headed towards the car. "See you at school tomorrow."

Christine watched as the car pulled out of the driveway. The cold damp air bristled on her skin and she could feel the wind picking up from across the harbour. She wished she could see the lighthouse from her front steps. With a sigh, she turned and walked inside.

Her father stood in the hallway.

"I told the McIntoshes I was sorry," Christine said, her eyes pleading for forgiveness. "Mack says that I shouldn't quit on their account. And then the Old Salt sang a song about a shipwreck ..." She realized she wasn't making any sense and she felt totally drained.

"I'll take your word for it, Chrissie. Now I think it's time that you get to bed," her father said. He gave her a hug and pointed her towards the stairs. Christine gave her mom a weary smile and headed upstairs.

Chapter Twenty-Two

A DECISION

*T*he next day, Christine watched for Scott at school. She was disappointed that she didn't see him but her thoughts were distracted by her concern for the lighthouse. At lunchtime, she phoned her mother nervously to find out how things were going.

"Still nothing yet, Chris," her mom replied. "But it's early. Don't forget there's the one-hour time difference between PEI and Ottawa. They're all just finishing their morning coffees."

Christine smiled at her mother's perpetual optimism. "Tell me again about what the person from the Heritage Department said yesterday. About today being the deadline," Christine persisted.

"She said that the Minister was hoping to have an answer from Cabinet today," Monica repeated, trying to reassure Christine. "They must be interested, though, or they wouldn't be taking such care to make sure they have all their i's dotted and their t's crossed."

Christine hoped her mother was right. Still, she fidgeted nervously all afternoon, constantly checking her watch, wondering what time the Cabinet meeting was being held. She imagined a roomful of important-looking people, in expensive suits, sitting around a gigantic table somewhere on Parliament Hill in Ottawa. What would they know about the wonders of the lighthouse?

Monica was waiting in the Jeep outside Queen Charlotte. Christine was surprised to see that Jennifer was there too.

"Your mom asked me to meet her here," Jennifer said, still refusing to make eye contact with Christine.

"I've got good news, girls," Monica Miller said, waving a fax in her hand. "But first, before we go to see the McIntoshes, I think the two of you need to talk." Monica climbed into the Jeep and pulled the door closed.

Christine and Jennifer looked at each other. The damp winter air cut through Christine's down-filled jacket and she pulled on the mittens that she had stuffed in her pocket. Finally, she decided to speak.

"It's my fault. I was an idiot. You had been so nice to me and I let you down," she sputtered.

There was another pause.

Jennifer finally looked her friend in the eyes. "I was wrong too," she said quietly. "I've gone to school with the same people and had the same friends forever. I can't imagine what it would be like to have to leave them."

Christine nodded. "I miss my friends from Ontario. Sometimes I wish I was still there. Other times I totally forget about them, and it's as if I've been here forever."

"You don't have to forget them," Jennifer replied softly.

"I know that now. And I'm sorry that I asked you to lie."

"It's okay. But you know what? I'm freezing!" Jennifer squealed and the two girls exchanged a quick hug, then quickly climbed into the waiting Jeep.

Monica Miller gave them a pleased look as the girls buckled up their seatbelts. "I think the two of you should be the ones to share the news with the McIntoshes in person."

Christine grabbed the fax from her mother and scanned it quickly. She let out a whoop of joy and handed the letter to Jennifer. "They've given the lighthouse historical building status," Christine exclaimed, beaming at her mother.

"So the lighthouse is saved, right?" Jennifer asked, skimming the letter that sported the official letterhead of the Minister of Heritage.

"Well, it means that the Coast Guard can't tear the lighthouse down," Monica explained. "Unfortunately, though, it doesn't really mean a lot of money for the project itself."

"We'll just have to raise the money to do the renovations," Christine answered, undaunted.

"My dad can round up a team of builders," Jennifer suggested. Christine nodded enthusiastically. Suddenly, she remembered her father's insistence that she quit the lighthouse project. She wondered how much Monica Miller had told him, and if he knew that Christine was going out to visit the McIntoshes again.

The Jeep pulled to a stop in front of the old lighthouse and the girls jumped out and ran for the door. Betty McIntosh was standing on the doorstep to greet them.

"Your mother said you had some news for us," Betty said kindly, escorting them into the parlour. She bustled around the room, taking their coats and getting them settled with mugs of hot chocolate and plates of cookies.

"Where's Mack?" Christine said, anxious to break the news.

Betty looked troubled. "He's feeling a bit under the weather, I'm afraid," she said in a quiet voice. "He hasn't been able to get out of bed today."

Christine was stunned. Mack had seemed in good spirits last night when she and Scott had visited. She realized now, though, that he had been quieter than usual, letting the Old Salt take centre stage. The news from Ottawa was forgotten, and Christine felt a lump growing in her throat.

"I wouldn't miss a visit from my favourite young ladies, missus," Mack boomed, appearing in the doorway.

Christine noticed immediately that something was wrong. Mack's white hair was rumpled and he had a gray, stubbly beard. His hands shook slightly as he settled into a rocking chair by the woodstove. His clothes seemed to hang loosely as if he had lost weight. The old lighthouse keeper was showing his eighty years.

"What's your news, lassie?" Mack said, his blue eyes sparkling with vigour, as if they alone could defy the aging process. The old man clutched the arm of the rocking chair, as if to hide his trembling hand.

Christine pulled the letter out of her pocket and waved it triumphantly in the air. "We got it," she exclaimed. "The lighthouse is now an official historical site. The Coast Guard can't touch it!"

"That's lovely, my dear," Betty said, giving Christine a hug. She went over and hugged Jennifer and then, Monica. Mack beamed triumphantly at all of them but he made no effort to get up.

"What does that mean, now, for all your plans?" Mack inquired.

"No money, I'm afraid," Monica replied. "But we think we can raise enough funds to get the project going. Then, hopefully, we can apply for grants and ask for contributions from tourists. Eventually, the idea is that as a national historic site, the lighthouse will pay for itself."

"So, we can stay here?" Betty asked, walking over to where her husband was sitting and carefully adjusting his sweater.

"We will have to set up a non-profit corporation to run the site and then we'll rent the place to you for a dollar a year," Monica answered.

"I think we can manage that," Mack said cheerfully. "For all your hard work, we thank you," he tilted his head in their direction, adding a wink to Christine and Jennifer.

They spent the next hour or so talking about their plans to get started on the restoration project. Monica showed the McIntoshes a sketch of the layout of the old shed and how it could be turned into a display house for the lighthouse memorabilia.

"We think we can have the display up and running by this summer," Christine told the McIntoshes enthusiastically. "And the Minister will even come back in person to unveil the plaque giving the Governors Lighthouse national heritage status."

Betty McIntosh nodded, then frowned as she looked over in her husband's direction. "Dave, dear, I think we have to get you back to bed," she said, noticing her husband's pallor.

"Yes, we should be leaving now," Monica hinted to the girls, getting up and putting on her coat.

"You've brought us wonderful news," Mack repeated, as he slowly got up from the rocking chair and shuffled towards the doorway. He grinned at Christine and Jennifer as he headed out of the room.

"Is he okay?" Monica asked, softly.

"I'm worried," Betty replied, keeping her voice hushed. "But this news should perk up his spirits."

On the ride back to Charlottetown, Christine was silent, staring out at the snow-covered fields, softly lit by the moon. The feeling of triumph over their success with the lighthouse was muted now, subdued by her growing concern over Mack's health.

Chapter Twenty-Three

MACK

Later that evening, Rob Miller was sitting in front of the television, flipping through the channels. Christine went in and sat on the couch.

"I'm sorry I was so difficult when you wanted to move here," she said quietly. Rob Miller put down the channel changer and looked at his daughter in surprise.

"Chrissie, that's ancient history now," he replied. "We can just forget about that now."

"No, you were right about this place and I was wrong," Christine persisted.

"Oh, I don't know that I was so right," her father shook his head. "In fact, I was being very selfish, dragging you and your mother halfway across the country, away from all your friends. I don't know what I was thinking. I guess my ego was hurt when I was laid off. You know, the crowd at the country club, the people on our street. I just thought they were all looking down at me. I felt I had to get out of there. This job came along and I jumped at it. It was that or ..." Her father couldn't finish the sentence and, for a moment, was lost in thought.

Christine was surprised. She was reminded how deeply hurt her father had been.

"I was so worried about what everyone else was thinking, I forgot to think about you," her father said, taking Christine's hand.

"But it has worked out," Christine said. "Mom loves it here and I'm even starting to like it," she added with a grin.

"Do you still want to go back to Ontario?" her father asked, again serious.

"I don't think so," Christine said, thoughtfully. "There are some things that I miss about Toronto. But the people here are nicer. And we've still got so much to do with the lighthouse."

"Ah yes, the lighthouse," her father said. "It always comes back to the lighthouse."

At supper, they had talked about the day's events, including their visit to share the good news with the McIntoshes. Rob Miller hadn't reprimanded his daughter then, but Christine had wondered what he was going to say.

"Chrissie, I'm proud of all the work you've done," he said, finally. "But we have to have some rules in this house. And you broke almost all of them when you took off for Toronto without telling us. Your work for the lighthouse is done now. At least you can feel like you're leaving them on a good note."

Christine felt tears welling up in her eyes and a lump in her throat. All she could do was nod.

The next day at school, Christine was surprised to see Scott waiting at her locker.

"I'm sorry I didn't get to talk to you yesterday," he said, somewhat bashfully. "I had to spend the day on the boat, giving my dad a hand with the traps."

"Then you haven't heard the news?" Christine exclaimed.

"What news?" Scott was puzzled.

"The lighthouse. We did it. We got the national historical status. It's saved!" Before she realized what she was doing, she grabbed Scott and gave him a hug. Then she turned a deep red as she noticed that some of the other students were watching and whispering.

"That's great," Scott answered, also looking a bit flustered. At the same time, Christine noticed that he leaned closer to her, with his shoulder still brushing against hers.

Scott's face grew worried though as Christine mentioned how tired Dave McIntosh had looked. "I hope he's okay," Scott said, suddenly serious. "He reminds me of my granddad," he added shyly.

"Was he a lighthouse keeper?" Christine asked.

"No, a lobster fisher, like my dad. But he had that same thick Island accent and he loved the sea," Scott replied. The buzzer rang and Christine fidgeted with her books, not sure what to do. She wanted to ask Scott more about his grandfather, but she knew that they both had to get to class.

"Well, I was wondering if you wanted to go out for coffee," Scott stammered. "And maybe we can go out and visit Mack sometime soon."

"Sure." Christine grinned with pleasure. Then she frowned slightly as she thought about her conversation with her father. He was right, though. The lighthouse project was basically over.

That evening the phone rang and Rob went to the kitchen to answer it. Christine waited nervously, wondering if it was Scott. However, when Rob returned to the living room, his face was grim.

"That was Betty McIntosh," he said. "Mack has had a stroke. They rushed him to the hospital this afternoon. It doesn't look good."

"Should we go to the hospital?" Christine asked.

Her father shook his head.

"I don't think that would be a good idea, Chrissie. He's in ICU right now and we'd just be in the way," her father replied kindly. "Mrs. McIntosh said that their children were on their way from Alberta."

"It must be really serious then," Christine whispered. "I should call Jennifer."

"It's lucky he didn't die before the ambulance arrived," Rob said to Monica as Christine left the room. Christine burst into tears as she ran upstairs to call her friend.

It was over a week before the doctors decided that Mack was going to pull through. As soon as the doctor gave the okay, Christine, Scott and Jennifer went to visit him at the Queen Elizabeth Hospital.

Betty McIntosh was outside the room and greeted them all with a hug.

"It's nice of you to come," she said kindly. "You'll find he's greatly changed," she warned them, glancing towards the room. "He can't speak at all but the doctors are hoping he'll eventually be able to write out his answers," she explained, her voice slightly shaky. "He won't walk again though," she said, her eyes welling up with tears. "And I'm afraid we won't be going back to our beloved lighthouse."

"What will you do?" Christine asked.

"We're going to move into a seniors' complex here in town," Betty answered, twisting a tissue in her hand. "They've promised us a view of the water," she added, smiling hopefully.

The young people were silent as they walked in the room where Mack was laying. The skin hung on his face. One of his hands lay twisted on his chest and his mouth was slightly uneven. But his blue eyes sparkled as he saw Christine, Scott and Jennifer come into the room. He made an attempt at speech but all that came out were muffled noises.

"Please sit down," Betty said, gesturing to the chairs near the bed. She went over to her husband and gently stroked his white hair into place.

Christine gazed over at the wall that was covered in photos of the lighthouse. There were old postcards featuring the Governors Light, some snapshots that Christine's mother had taken for the project and the photograph of Betty and Dave McIntosh on their wedding day.

"They're starting to work on the repairs at the lighthouse," Scott jumped in, seeing that Mack was watching them intently.

"Christine and I want to work there this summer," Jennifer added. "Christine's mom is applying for a government grant to pay our salaries and so we can spend the summer helping Christine's mom go through all the lighthouse stuff you've collected. Hopefully by next summer, we'll be able to turn it into an exhibit in the old shed," Jennifer continued. Then, she fell silent as she realized that the old couple would never be returning to their home.

"It sounds wonderful," Betty smiled. She had been staying in town with her cousin and had been out to the lighthouse only once since Mack's stroke. Since she didn't drive, there was no way for her to stay in their old home.

"But it won't be the same without you," Christine said to Mack. "Without you, there would be no lighthouse." Her eyes were filling with tears.

Mack made another movement as if to answer her but no words would come out. Betty changed the subject, asking the girls how their parents were doing. After a few more minutes, the young people got up to go.

Christine went over to the bed and leaned over Mack to give him a gentle kiss on the cheek. "Thank you for everything," she said through her tears. Jennifer stood on the other side of the bed, holding the old lightkeeper's hand. Her eyes were also brimming over with tears, which she tried to wipe away before Mack could see. Standing at the door, Scott stared out the window, clenching his lips together.

Outside in the hallway, Betty clutched Christine's hand. "Don't be sad, my dear," she said, softly. "You've given him so much happiness over the last few months. You saved our home and now his lighthouse will live forever. We'll be fine in town, don't you worry," Betty reassured them.

"But he's never lived anywhere else," Christine sobbed.

"Yes, but at least he's still living," the old woman replied. She encouraged the three of them to come visit them soon in their new apartment. "On a clear day, we can see straight out the harbour, all the way to our light."

The three teenagers were silent as they walked out of the hospital.

"She's right, you know," Scott said finally. "The two of you did a good thing, rallying everyone to save that lighthouse. That gave him the will to live, I think."

Christine shrugged her shoulders. "I'd rather have him back healthy, the way he was." They climbed into the Jeep where Monica Miller was waiting. At least he knows his lighthouse is safe now, Christine thought to herself.

Chapter Twenty-Four

ON BOARD
THE CHRISTOPHER ROBIN

Scott had hockey practice that night, but he and Christine agreed that they would go for coffee the following evening. Christine imagined what Allie and Brittany would say. I'm going on a date with the son of a lobster fisher, she giggled to herself. She felt suddenly guilty as she realized it had been a couple of days since she had spoken to her friends in Toronto. The girls had promised to stay in touch after Brittany's birthday, but they were all so busy. Christine wondered if they would understand her excitement about the success with the lighthouse project. Allie would, and even Brittany had seemed interested when they were talking about the lighthouse on the way to the airport.

The next day seemed to drag on. Christine kept an eye out for Scott at school but she didn't see him. When Jennifer asked what she was doing that night, Christine hummed and hawed. Jennifer burst out laughing.

"You're going out on a date, aren't you?" she giggled. "I've never seen such a poor job of hiding the truth in my life. Why didn't you just tell me?"

"Oh, it's not a date, as such," Christine protested. That made Jennifer laugh even harder.

"That Scott MacFarlane certainly has you blushing, my girl," Jennifer smiled, nudging Christine in the ribs.

It was early evening by the time Scott arrived at the Miller house. Christine dashed out the door, waving goodbye to her parents. She and Scott followed the boardwalk, past the hotel where she and her family had stayed, to the marina. Scott pointed her towards the piers.

Because it was past the end of the sailing season, there were only a few boats left in the marina. Most of the finger piers had already been lifted from the water and were piled up for the season. Christine noticed a musty odour of seaweed and fish.

Scott led her down the ramp and along the pier to a white fishing boat called the CHRISTOPHER ROBIN. It was a stocky-looking boat, with a wide-open deck out back and a covered cabin up front.

"They're flat out back because they need to carry hundred of lobster traps," Scott explained. "Don't worry. They're the most seaworthy ship you'll find."

Scott took Christine's hand and helped her climb aboard.

"What are those?" she asked, pointing to two large orange suits, sitting on the edge of one deck.

"Survival suits," Scott replied, giving her a mysterious smile. "We've got our coffee to go tonight. You drink it black, right?"

Christine gazed at Scott in amazement. What was he up to?

It was the first time Christine had been on one of the fishing boats. "Isn't it a little cold out there?" she asked looking out at the lonely waters of the harbour.

"Here, put this on," Scott urged. He showed her how to pull on the giant orange survival suit. It was thick like a gigantic life jacket and it had all sorts of special tabs and zippers. Scott grinned as Christine snapped up the final closure.

"Yes, you look like a real Island girl now." He laughed.

"I didn't realize that you had wear this kind of clothing to have coffee on PEI," Christine teased.

"It all depends on where you're drinking your coffee, I guess," Scott answered with a wink.

He silently flicked a number of switches and a loud diesel motor roared to life.

"You'll have to push me off the dock," he shouted over the noise of the engine. Scott efficiently untied the lines along the side of the CHRISTOPHER ROBIN. He showed Christine how to push off the dock on his signal. With a burst of diesel fumes, the boat chugged its way out of the marina.

Christine stood next to Scott in the cabin as the fishing boat made its way across the Charlottetown harbour. Though it was late fall, the evening was quite balmy. There was not a hint of breeze and the water was almost glassy. The sun had already disappeared and darkness was falling. The harbour was empty except for their boat.

Without a word, Scott carefully steered the boat towards the Governors Light. Christine turned to him when she realized where they were going. Scott gave her another wink.

It only took about ten minutes for them to make their way through the neck of the harbour to the shore alongside the lighthouse. Scott put the engine into neutral, went to the back of the boat and dropped an anchor overboard with a splash. Then he silenced the noisy diesel.

Christine turned and gazed at the lighthouse. It loomed above them, the flashing light almost unbearably bright. Scott handed Christine her coffee.

"I hope it's still warm enough," Scott murmured.

"It's wonderful," Christine stammered. "I mean, the lighthouse is. The coffee's okay too."

They both laughed.

"I didn't think you'd seen it yet from the water," Scott explained. "You can see now how it was such an important guide for anyone out on the water. I've been out with my father and had bad weather roll in. But you could always see the light."

"Why would they want to tear it down?" Christine shook her head.

"It's progress, I guess," Scott shrugged. "Now we've got this handy GPS gizmo. That's global positioning system. It gives you your location from a satellite. But, you know, I still feel better knowing I can see the light."

Christine nodded. She thought about Mack lying silent in the hospital bed, a boat's ride away from his beloved home. She wished he and Betty would be able to go home someday. Only then would things be right.

Christine and Scott stood, lost in silence for a moment. Then Scott carefully took her coffee cup. Before she knew what was happening, he leaned over and kissed her. The light flashed above them, reflecting off their orange survival suits. Christine closed her eyes and could feel her heart pounding in rhythm to the pulse of the lighthouse beam.

The two teenagers were quiet on their way back to the marina. Scott pulled Christine close to the wheel, as he steered the CHRISTOPHER ROBIN through the dark waters of the harbour. Christine could not imagine a more perfect first date. She sent a silent "thank you" to the lighthouse. Again, its powerful force had changed her life.

Chapter Twenty-Five

THE OLD SALT'S STORY

*O*ver the next couple of weeks, Christine was caught up in a blur of exams and preparations for Christmas. Mack was still in the hospital but the doctors hoped that he would be able to leave before Christmas. Christine and Jennifer tried to visit as often as they could but the old man tired quickly.

Jennifer and Christine handed in their lighthouse project to Ms. Carpenter, who received their thick binder with a smile.

Once exams were over, Christine spent most of her time with Scott. They went Christmas shopping, and Scott invited Christine to his hockey game.

The afternoon before the game, Christine was in her room wrapping presents when the phone rang. It was Allie, calling from Toronto.

"What's up, Chrissie?" Allie asked. "How's it going with Scott?"

Not long after her first date with Scott, Christine had called her friends. They had been impressed when she told them the story of her date on the CHRISTOPHER ROBIN. At first Christine had been somewhat reluctant to tell them too much about it. She thought they would think it tacky to go on a date on a fishing boat. But their reaction was exactly the opposite. The girls had been so eager that Christine had described it all in detail, though she did skip over the kiss.

"That is sooooo romantic," Allie had squealed when Christine finished her story. "He sounds so nice. Why aren't there guys like that at North Park?"

Now, two weeks later, Christine told Allie that she was going to Scott's hockey game that night.

"Sounds like fun," Allie remarked. "So, guess what Brittany's up to now?"

Christine immediately realized that this was probably the real reason Allie was calling. "This is Brittany we're talking about. I can hardly guess," she said, rolling her eyes.

"She's back together with that jerk Martin Drake," Allie replied, pausing to give Christine a moment to react. "I guess she just couldn't stand not having a boyfriend."

Christine suddenly felt sorry for her old friend. If she had been back in Toronto, she and Allie would have hung around together until Brittany decided to pay attention to them again. But now Allie was on her own.

"That's too bad," Christine answered, her voice filled with genuine sympathy. "Hey — why don't you come out and visit me sometime in the New Year?" she suggested.

Allie sounded grateful. "I'd love to, Chrissie, but I'm going to be super busy with the basketball team this season. I made the AA team and we're travelling to a whole bunch of tournaments, and even to the States."

Christine was astonished. Allie had quit basketball last year after Brittany had teased her about it. Now it appeared she was ready to do what she wanted, not what Brittany told her to do.

"That's super," Christine said. "You're a great basketball player. And you made AA in Grade Nine! That's awesome."

"I won't get much playing time," Allie replied sheepishly. "But maybe I can come visit you this summer."

"Sure. The lighthouse will be an official historic site by then," Christine added. The girls chatted for a few more minutes but then it was time for Christine to head over to the hockey arena for Scott's game.

"Thanks for calling, Allie," Christine said before hanging up. "And hang in there. You know what Brittany is like. Hot one day, cold the next."

"Yeah sure," Allie answered. "And, Chrissie, I miss you."

As she changed into a sweater and jeans for the game, Christine wondered what she would have been doing now if she had still been living her old life in Toronto. Probably not going to a hockey game, she giggled to herself.

"Oh, this is serious, when he invites you to his game," Jennifer teased as they lined up for tickets to get into the Simmons Arena, just across the parking lot from their school. Jennifer had advised Christine to dress warmly. "It'll be almost as cold as outdoors," she warned.

Christine looked around the small arena with amazement. The only hockey rink she had ever been to was the Air Canada Centre in Toronto, just after it opened. She had been impressed by the fancy corporate box where she and her dad had sat with other men in suits from his company and a few of their children. They had been treated to a steady stream of food and all the ice cream they wanted. There were four television sets in the box, and everyone received an autographed team photo when they left the sparkling new arena. In contrast, the Simmons rink had creaky wooden stands and chipped paint.

"They have to be careful how they hit the boards," Jennifer joked. "The whole place might collapse!"

Jennifer seemed to know almost everyone at the arena that night. As they walked to their seats, they passed a long line of men leaning over the railing of a walkway high above the stands. Almost every one of them wore a hockey jacket and some sort of baseball cap. "How's it goin' now, Jenn?" one of them shouted at the girls. Jennifer gave him a friendly wave. She stopped and introduced Christine to a couple of her father's friends.

"So you're the girl from away? The one with the lighthouse ideas," one of them said in a thick Island accent. Christine nodded shyly. She was startled that the man knew who she was. At the same time, she was impressed by the friendly camaraderie of everyone at the rink. It was like a party.

Looking around her, Christine was amazed to see the stands almost full. There were people of all ages, ranging from grandmotherly women to babies bundled up in snowsuits, being carried around in their car seats. Young kids scrambled up and down the bleachers, racing to the canteen for fries dripping in ketchup and cups of steaming hot chocolate.

"Why are there so many people here?" Christine asked.

"Hockey is a way of life here," Jennifer replied, only half-joking. "Islanders love their hockey. And they take it very seriously."

As they took her seats, Christine suddenly felt very conspicuous. She wondered how many people knew that she was dating Scott MacFarlane. She was so used to the anonymity of her life in Toronto. There, no one had time to get to know their neighbours. It was exactly the opposite here on Prince Edward Island.

She looked around the rink again and spotted Scott's brother Doug, and a man she assumed was Scott's father. Doug caught her eye and gave her a quick wave. Oh no, she thought, now his dad's going to be watching me too.

Suddenly, the door opened and a parade of players dressed in red, white and black rushed onto the ice, to the cheers of the crowd. Christine strained to catch a glimpse of Scott. She knew that he was number 8 on his team, the Charlottetown Abbies.

Christine tried to enjoy her first Island hockey experience but found herself distracted. She hadn't expected such a big crowd, and she was astonished too at how much they yelled at the players and especially at the referee. Beside her, Jennifer jumped up and down out of her seat, cheering for some of the guys that she knew from school. Christine just watched in silence, too self-conscious to move.

"Scott's really good," she said to Jennifer, after the first period.

"He is good," Jennifer agreed. "And he doesn't have a big ego about it. Some of those hockey players ..." Jennifer just shook her head. Christine wasn't sure what she meant and felt too dumb to ask.

The Abbies won the game 3-1 over their rivals from Summerside and the delighted crowd poured out of the rink, everyone in great spirits. Christine felt very conspicuous as she and Jennifer waited outside the door to the dressing room with all of the parents and girlfriends and even a few autograph seekers.

"Can't we wait somewhere less obvious?" Christine whispered.

"Don't worry. They're all looking at the hockey players. They won't even notice us," Jennifer replied.

Scott came out of the dressing room door, his hair still wet. He gave Jennifer and Christine a shy wave.

"So what did you think, Christine?" he asked. Christine felt her face growing warmer.

"It was fun," she said, then realized that she sounded less than enthusiastic. "I mean, you were great. Your team was great."

Scott and Jennifer laughed.

"Do you want to go to Little Christo's?" Scott asked.

The girls nodded.

"Do you mind if Mike Arsenault comes along?" Scott added. Christine was surprised to see Jennifer blushing.

The four teenagers walked up Kirkwood to the popular pizza place on University Avenue. As they squeezed into the booth, the three Islanders continued analyzing the game. Christine felt as if they were speaking a foreign language.

"Did you see that wicked 2-on-1 in the second? I can't believe you missed that shot, Scotty," Mike Arsenault teased. He was a tall, wide-shouldered boy from Grade 10. He was one of the top scorers on the Abbies and one of the most popular players. Christine had heard Scott mention his name before.

"What was with that penalty in the third period?" Jennifer asked, and she and Mike resumed an animated discussion of the game. Christine sat listening to them, feeling left out. She resolved to pay more attention to hockey in the future. I might as well try to fit in, she thought to herself.

"Did you really like it?" Scott asked Christine.

"I've only ever been to see the Maple Leafs," Christine explained sheepishly. "I didn't realize the Abbies were such a big thing."

"It's a small place." Scott shrugged. "People don't have much to do in the winter. So most of the guys play hockey. And, yeah, in a big town, you'd never get his kind of a crowd for a bantam game."

"Oh, I forgot to tell you, Christine," Jennifer suddenly interjected. "My dad told me an interesting story the other day about the Old Salt."

Christine turned to Jennifer, instantly intrigued. The old sailor was often at the hospital when they went to visit Mack. According to Betty, the two old men would often sit for hours in front of the window in the hospital room, staring out towards the water. The Old Salt strummed his guitar and even sang a few ballads when the spirit moved him, much to the delight of the other patients.

"What did your dad say?" Christine urged her friend on.

"My dad knows the Old Salt from his fishing days. His real name is Walter Bernard, and his family is originally from the Malpeque Bay area," Jennifer began.

Scott told Christine that Malpeque Bay was just outside Summerside, on the Gulf of St. Lawrence. "It's a big mussel-fishing area," he added. "In the summer, the bay is filled with long rows of white buoys. The mussels grow in a kind of sock, hanging off the buoys. That's so they don't get all sandy," he explained. "And they have fine oysters out that way, too."

Jennifer resumed her story. "According to my father, a couple of years ago, one of the Old Salt's brothers was out fishing with his two sons. They were fishing for mussels. The boat they were on was a new design they were trying out. It was flat, with more room to put the mussels on. But a storm came up and the boat capsized." She paused.

Christine's eyes grew wide with horror. This sounded like one of the Old Salt's stories of the old shipwrecks, but this happened just a few years ago.

"What happened?" Scott asked urgently. Mike leaned in closer, obviously eager to hear the rest of the story.

"None of them knew how to swim," Jennifer said sadly. "They weren't even wearing lifejackets. Not a lot of the fisher-men do. The water was so cold. They all drowned before help could get there."

The teenagers fell silent. The waiter came up with their pizza and placed it in front of them. But suddenly no one was hungry.

"How can he still tell those stories?" Christine asked. "Why doesn't he hate the sea now?"

Jennifer shrugged. "It's one of those things that's happened to so many families here."

"It happens a lot out where my family's from, up West," Mike added.

"I guess everyone knows that's one of the risks you take when you fish," Scott agreed, in a thoughtful voice. "I worry about my dad, and about Doug."

After a moment's pause, the conversation switched back to the hockey game and the teenagers dug into the pizza. Christine listened to her friends, as she tried to shake off the gloom of the story about the Old Salt's lost relatives. While she had always been captivated by the beauty of the lighthouses, she realized now how important they must have been for Islanders. No one could have saved those mussel fishers, she thought sadly. But there must have been many others who made it to shore safely because of the big, old lights.

Chapter Twenty-Six

MORE BAD NEWS

*C*hristmas flew past and by mid-January, Monica was working full-time on the lighthouse project. She was the chairperson of the non-profit corporation set up to run the Governors Light.

Despite all the public attention that the project had received, the fund-raising to start renovation was going slowly. Christine listened anxiously to her mother's growing frustration.

"The government agencies will only match whatever private contributions we can raise," she explained. "And there are really no big companies here to make corporate donations."

"I've done my best," her husband said. "Our fund-raising committee said they would consider donating money next fiscal year. But they're already over their contribution limits for this year. The timing just isn't great, Monica."

He smiled at his wife encouragingly.

She ran her fingers through her hair and growled at the numbers on the notepad in front of her. "It's just not going to work," she said, anxiously. "We've got to find some other option."

Christine reported her parents' conversation to Jennifer at lunch the next day at school.

"That's the trouble the historical society runs into all the time," Jennifer said, shaking her head. "There just aren't enough dollars to go around. It's a poor place, in many ways."

"So, what now?" Christine asked, taking a bite of her sandwich.

Melanie sat down at their table. "What are you talking about?" she asked. Though Christine never felt totally accepted by Jennifer's other friends, they now seemed to accept Christine, particularly since she started going out with Scott MacFarlane.

"Oh, just the trouble they're having raising money for the lighthouse renovations," Christine replied. She didn't think Melanie was very interested in the lighthouse.

"Well, my father may be able to help out," Melanie said.

Christine turned to Jennifer to see if she knew what Melanie was talking about. Jennifer looked just as puzzled as Christine.

"He wants somewhere to expand his cottages, and we were talking the other day about the lighthouse. He thought it would be the perfect place to put a new cottage development. The lighthouse would be sure to attract the tourists," Melanie explained. Then she lowered her voice to a whisper. "But he doesn't want anyone to get there first. So don't breathe a word about this. Otherwise his competitors will be right in there too."

Christine was too shocked to say a word. She wondered if her mother had heard about this plan. She could imagine her mom's reaction. Monica Miller was already critical of the way the Island was being overrun by tourist development without properly preserving its heritage sites. Putting cottages up at the lighthouse would be the last thing she would support.

"What do you think?" she asked Jennifer, after Melanie and the rest of the girls picked up their trays and left the cafeteria, leaving the two friends alone.

"I don't know. Maybe it's the only way," Jennifer shrugged.

"What's the only way?" Scott asked, pulling a chair up next to Christine. They filled him in on what Melanie had told them.

"That's a super idea," Scott said. "Don't you think so?"

Christine looked troubled. "I don't know. I mean I don't want the lighthouse to end up looking like Cavendish." She and her parents had visited the famous Island tourist destination a couple of weekends after they arrived on PEI. Her mother had been excited about visiting the Green Gables house exhibit, which was all about Lucy Maud Montgomery, the author of the Anne books. However, when the Millers drove into the community, they had been turned off by all the tee-shirt shops and theme parks in the area, including one that featured an imitation space shuttle for kids.

"What's wrong with Cavendish?" Scott asked her, a defensive tone sneaking into his voice. "That's what the people from away want. Something to do when they come to PEI."

"I didn't say there was anything wrong with the place," Christine replied, also getting defensive. "It's just kind of tacky. That space ship, for example. What does it have to do with PEI?"

"And what else do you find tacky?" Scott persisted. "I guess our rink is kind of rundown compared to the Air Canada Centre."

"No, you're taking this the wrong way," Christine protested. "I just don't want the lighthouse to turn into a big tourism trap."

"What's a trap to you is a job creation project to us," Scott said coldly. "Jobs matter here. Saving the lighthouse matters. If this is the way to do it, who cares if there are a couple of cottages around or not? We're not all made of money." He turned to Jennifer looking for support.

"I think the cottage idea is worth a try," Jennifer replied. "The important thing is to save the lighthouse, right?"

The bell rang, and Scott muttered something about giving Christine a call later but she could tell that he was still upset.

Christine turned to Jennifer. "Why is he so mad at me? What did I say?"

Jennifer shook her head. " I guess he felt you were criticizing Islanders. Some of the hockey players were ribbing him about dating a girl from away. From Toronto. You know — as if you were some kind of snob or something. One of them asked him if you had given him a cell phone. I guess they still remember that day in class."

Christine rolled her eyes. "They still remember that? That was ages ago. And when are they going to forget that I'm from Toronto and just treat me like everyone else?"

Scott avoided her for the rest of the day, and when she checked the answering machine at home, no one had called. Christine's heart sank.

At supper, Monica Miller was in a fury. She waved a piece of paper at her husband across the table. "The nerve of this guy Redmond. He wants to lease the lighthouse for one dollar a year. In exchange, he'll turn it into a tourism development with twenty-five cottages scattered around the property. Yes, that would be a sweet deal. One dollar for all that shorefront property. He says he would be doing us a favour, preserving the lighthouse. Meanwhile, I have the Coast Guard breathing down my neck. I have to take over possession of the place in three weeks, and as of right now, I have about five thousand dollars to do the renovations."

"What about the McIntoshes?" Christine said. "The whole idea was to make sure that they got to stay in the lighthouse. Remember? That was where this all started."

Her father shook his head sadly. "It just isn't realistic for them to stay out there on their own now. Maybe this is the best option, Monica."

"It sounds like a money grab by this Redmond. Where is the heritage value in a cottage development?" Monica sighed. "I'll talk to him and see what else he has to offer. I just hate the idea of that beautiful spot turning into a tacky tourism development, like those places around Cavendish. You know, with the 'Anne Shirley Pizzeria' and the 'Matthew and Marilla Laundromat'."

The Millers all laughed, but Christine noticed that her mom still looked worried.

Later that night, Scott called Christine to apologize. "I guess I flew off the handle there," he mumbled.

"I'm sorry too if I said something that was insulting to Islanders. I didn't mean to," Christine replied. "I just don't want someone to ruin the lighthouse."

"Christine, I don't think we should discuss this. We obviously have to agree to disagree," Scott cautioned. Christine wasn't totally satisfied with his answer, but agreed not to pursue it.

A week later, Scott was over at Christine's house for supper. As they were sitting down to eat, the phone rang.

"I'm expecting a call," Monica said, running to answer the phone. She returned with an excited look on her face.

"I've got some news," she told them as she cut a piece of lasagna and put it on a plate for Scott. "The board of the lighthouse committee and I had a meeting with Mr. Redmond this afternoon. He has made some concessions and has agreed to the terms that we asked for. It looks as though we have a deal."

"Congratulations," Rob cheered, raising his glass in a toast.

Christine frowned. She looked over at Scott, who gave her an encouraging smile.

"Christine, it's for the best," her mother continued, noticing her daughter's reaction.

"Am I the only one who doesn't think this is a good idea?" Christine asked. "You've agreed to let him build tourist cottages?"

"Yes, but he has agreed to maintain the main structure of the lighthouse. We just weren't going to have enough money to save it, Chrissie. It was in much worse shape than we thought. This was our only hope."

"When do they get it?" Christine asked finally.

"Get what?" Monica asked.

"Get the lighthouse," Christine snapped at her mother.

"They're starting work on the cottages right away. They want them to be ready for June ..." her mother began.

"I want to go there now," Christine interrupted. "I want to see it one more time before they wreck it."

"Christine, they're not going to wreck it," her mother protested. However, she reluctantly agreed to drive Christine and Scott to the lighthouse after supper.

Scott said very little as the Millers ate. When he and Christine went to get their jackets on, he grabbed her arm.

"Your mother has worked really hard to get this deal. I think you should be happy for her," he said quietly.

"I can't be happy about some tacky cottages being built next to that beautiful lighthouse," Christine replied, grabbing her arm away.

"It's not your lighthouse. If it belongs to anyone, it belongs to Mack and Betty. And they're just happy that it's not going to fall to pieces."

"It was not going to fall to pieces."

"Christine, you have to wake up and smell the coffee on this one. This is the best thing that could happen."

"Are you two ready to go?" Monica asked, grabbing her keys. Christine and Scott glared at each other.

"I think I'll just head home," Scott said politely. "I can see the cottages another time," he added pointedly.

Christine sullenly walked to the Jeep and got into the passenger side without saying anther word to Scott. She and Monica drove up North River Road in silence.

When they pulled up to the lighthouse, they found a crew of men packing up boxes and moving them out of the old tool shed. Jennifer's dad was among them.

"What are they doing?" Christine asked her mother sharply.

"We have to tear down the shed. It's too far gone to save it," her mother said sadly. "Your father made arrangements to put the lighthouse artifacts into storage, at least until we can find some place to put them."

Christine put her face in her hands. She couldn't believe what she was hearing. When she looked over towards the woods, she noticed neon orange markers and stakes where the new cottages were going to be built.

"Forget it," she said in a monotone voice. "Let's go."

Christine refused to look back as they pulled out of the driveway and the lighthouse disappeared from sight.

Chapter Twenty-Seven

BRITTANY

*A*fter school the next day, Christine was surprised to see her dad's car in the driveway when she got home. Her heart jumped to her throat. Her mind raced through the possibilities of what had happened. Was it Mack? Had her dad lost his job again? Where was her mother? By the time she got in the door, she was shaking.

"Sit down, Christine," Rob Miller said seriously, taking Christine's hand in his.

"There's been a car accident in Toronto. It's Brittany."

Christine caught her breath. Monica rushed in the door. He exchanged a worried look with his wife. She came over and put her arm around her daughter's shoulders.

"How bad?" Christine asked, her voice shaking.

"She's in intensive care but at least she's conscious now. Her face was badly cut up. They've had a plastic surgeon in. They're hoping that she'll make a full recovery. Right now it's wait and see," her father concluded.

"What should I do?" Christine asked, turning back to her parents.

"If you want, you can go to Toronto. I can cash in some of my bonus points," Rob offered gently.

Christine still clung to his hand but she had sunk onto the bench by the door. She quickly went upstairs and called Allie.

"Allie, what happened?" Christine asked when her friend answered.

"Chrissie. You've got to come home," Allie said, her voice shaking. She told Christine what she knew about the accident. "Chrissie, it's so awful. They don't know if she'll ..." Her friend couldn't say any more.

Christine promised to call back when she had talked to her parents. She hung up the phone and started to sob. After a few minutes, she heard her parents tentatively knock. Christine opened the door, clutching a handful of tissues.

"I think I'd like to go see her," she whispered. Her parents nodded. "I'd better get packed."

A few minutes later, the phone rang in. Christine thought it was Allie phoning back.

"Hi. I just heard what happened. Your mom called me." Scott's voice caught Christine off-guard. "I'm sorry about your friend," he continued.

Christine tried to hold back the tears. "I'm going to Toronto tomorrow. To see her."

"We'll have to talk when you get back," Scott told her. There was an awkward pause. "I hope she's okay," Scott said. "Take care, Christine. Okay?"

Christine tossed and turned all that night. She was haunted by images of her friend lying in a hospital room, covered in bandages from head to foot like a mummy. In her nightmare, Brittany couldn't move. Christine was filled with horror as she realized that the hospital bed had turned into the deck of an old sailing ship. The winds started to whip the ship's sails, which broke away from the mast. Brittany lay moaning on the deck and was tossed and turned violently by the waves. Christine tried to scream as the mast fell and Brittany was thrown into the churning waters. She turned on the light and sat up, staring out the window for the rest of the night.

The next morning, Christine was sitting on the front steps when Jennifer arrived at the Miller house. She sat down beside Christine.

"I talked to my friend Allie last night," Christine said, her voice trembling. "Brittany was driving the car. The accident was her fault."

Jennifer looked surprised. She knew that Brittany was four-teen, too young to drive. She waited for Christine to continue.

"And that's not the worst part. Her boyfriend was in the car too and he may never walk again," Christine's voice trailed off into a whisper.

"Christine, I'm sorry. Was he a friend of yours too?" Jennifer asked.

Christine winced slightly at her question. She had been too embarrassed to tell Jennifer what had happened with Martin Drake in Toronto.

"No, not a friend but I knew him," she replied cryptically.

The Millers came out of the house, carrying Christine's suitcase. "Time to go, Chrissie."

"Can you go and visit Mack for me?" Christine asked Jennifer. "I promised to come and see him this weekend. But please ask Betty not to tell him about the cottages. I want to be there when she tells him."

Jennifer nodded, though she looked confused.

"And, please, don't tell him about what happened to Brittany." Her voice was starting to shake again.

As she waved goodbye to Jennifer, Christine realized that she hadn't told her friend what Scott had said. What did he want to talk about? More bad news, she thought, feeling her eyes starting to fill up with tears. Well, he would have to wait until she got back.

After she hugged her parents and boarded the small plane for the trip to Halifax, Christine started to imagine what lay ahead in Toronto. She tried not to think about what Brittany would look like in the hospital bed. Instead, she played over in her mind the scenes from her last trip to Ontario. So much had happened since then. She shuddered as she recalled her encounter with Martin Drake. He had been a jerk but she felt guilty now as she thought of him lying paralyzed in a hospital bed. She wondered how Brittany was dealing with that.

Allie was waiting at the airport when Christine arrived. Christine was shocked at her friend's appearance. Though Allie looked more athletic than ever in a North Park track suit and runners, the strain of the last couple of days was written all over her face. Her clothes and hair looked disheveled. She grabbed Christine in a big bear hug.

"I'm so glad you're here, even if it's just for a few days," she whispered.

"How is she?" Christine asked.

Allie shrugged. "Typical Brittany in some ways. Her parents are most worried about making sure they get the best plastic surgeon. She doesn't seem to be reacting at all," Allie explained.

"What about Martin?" Christine asked tentatively.

"Well, his football playing days are over, but they're pretty sure he's going to be okay now," Allie replied.

"He isn't paralyzed?" Christine said, surprised.

"Oh, he was but he's okay now," Allie answered. Then she looked troubled. "You don't know about Brittany, do you?" she asked.

"Know what? I just know what you told me," Christine replied tensely. She was angry with herself that she had wasted her time feeling sorry for Martin Drake.

"It's Brittany who has the serious leg damage," Allie said slowly. "I guess a bone in her leg was shattered so badly they couldn't totally repair it. She'll walk with a limp, once she can finally walk again."

Christine felt her stomach lurch at the news, as she and her friend made their way in silence to the car. Christine was surprised to see Allie's parents waiting to drive them to the hospital. Mr. and Mrs. O'Donnell smiled at Christine as she got in the car. On the way to the hospital, Allie's parents asked her a couple of questions about Prince Edward Island. She answered politely but they seemed to sense from her half-hearted replies that she didn't really want to talk. They drove the rest of the way in silence.

Christine tried to imagine how Brittany was feeling. She had always been so worried about her appearance and what people thought of her. How was she going to take this news?

The O'Donnells stopped in front of the hospital. Mrs. O'Donnell turned to the girls in the back seat. "Take as long as you need," she said, looking from one girl to the other, as if she were trying to assess how they were doing. She gave her daughter a comforting smile. "We'll meet you back here at five o'clock."

Allie turned to Christine as they walked up to the sliding doors at the main entrance. "My mom and dad have been great," she said. "They've been driving me back and forth. My dad even took time off work to help me go pick up some things for Brittany."

"What am I going to say to her?" Christine gulped, stopping in the lobby. She sat down in one of the chairs in the waiting area. She couldn't go any further. She wasn't ready to face Brittany yet.

Allie looked at her friend. "Just be yourself," she replied and gave Christine an encouraging smile.

"What was Brittany doing driving?" Christine whispered, turning to Allie, who had sat down beside her and was staring off into the distance.

"It was Martin's idea, I guess," Allie said, lowering her voice. "She had been bragging at some party about what a great driver she was. He threw her the keys and dared her to drive them home."

Christine shook her head. She thought of all the times that she had been subjected to one of Brittany's stubborn streaks. She knew that once she had been dared, there was no way that Brittany would have backed down. Maybe she honestly believed she could drive.

"Let's get this over with," Allie sighed, getting up and heading to the elevator. When they got to the ward, Christine stalled for time, telling Allie she needed to go to the washroom first. Christine stood staring at the mirror, trying to steel her courage to face her friend. I've got to do this, she thought to herself. I can't cry in front of Brittany, she resolved. She closed her eyes for a minute and tried to imagine she was back on the Island. But no images would come.

"Chrissie!" Brittany exclaimed as Christine finally walked in the door. Allie had settled into a chair beside the bed and was reading *Cosmo*. Christine went over to the bed and tentatively hugged Brittany.

"I'm not going to break," Brittany scolded her. "Sit," she commanded, patting a spot on the bed beside her. Brittany's blonde hair hung limply around her pale face, which was still covered in bandages. Her arms were cut and bruised and one leg was in a cast.

"How are things in PEI?" Brittany asked.

"Good," Christine said, not sure what to say next.

"What happened to that lighthouse?"

Christine was surprised that her friend remembered the lighthouse project. She gave Brittany a brief update, trying to sound excited about the new cottage development. She hesitated slightly as she told Brittany about Mack and his stroke.

Her friend's face grew sombre. "I can't imagine not being able to talk," Brittany said with a quick smile. Then her face grew serious again. "I guess you've heard about my bum leg," Brittany's voice was strained as she tried to sound upbeat.

"It doesn't matter, Brittany," Christine whispered.

"I know it doesn't." Brittany took Christine's hand. "I'm lucky, I guess. It could have been worse. I was so stupid." Brittany shuddered slightly. "I let him talk me into it. And I should have just said no …"

"It's all over now," Christine said, distressed at seeing her friend in so much pain. Brittany closed her eyes and sank back into the pillow.

"Tell me again what that lighthouse is like," Brittany said softly.

Christine carefully described the red and white striped tower, and the way the walls narrowed as you went up the stairs from floor to floor. She told her about the trapdoor and the way the light almost blinded you as it flashed past on its regular rhythm. Christine could almost feel the salty air on her face as she pretended to take Brittany out onto the narrow balcony overlooking the Charlottetown Harbour, with the fast tidal currents swelling past, to and fro, pulled by the powers of the moon. A slight smile formed on Brittany's bruised face and a look of calm spread over her.

A few minutes later the nurse came in to tell them that it was time for Brittany to rest.

"We'll be back later in a couple of hours, Brittany. Any special requests?" Allie asked.

"Can you get me a picture of a lighthouse?" she asked Christine, who nodded in reply. "And, Chrissie. I'm glad you came home."

When the two girls got out the door, Allie grabbed Christine's arm. "That was the first time she has talked about the accident," she said urgently.

"What do you mean?" Christine asked, puzzled.

"Until now, she has never, ever, mentioned her leg," Allie explained. "She just refuses to talk about it. With the doctors or anyone."

"I don't get it," Christine replied.

"Your story about the old lighthouse keeper. I think that really struck home for her," Allie said thoughtfully. "I guess, in a way, she was holding everything inside until you got here. It means a lot to her."

Christine was amazed by her friend's comments. She had always assumed that she needed Brittany more than Brittany needed her.

The girls spent the next couple of hours combing a bookstore near the hospital for posters and books about lighthouses. They weren't able to find a lot, but enough to put up on Brittany's wall at the hospital.

As they made their way back to the hospital, Christine finally decided to ask Allie the question that had been nagging at her ever since she heard about the accident.

"Allie, I don't want to be mean or anything, but why would Brittany have done this? She didn't know how to drive. I mean, she's only fourteen. And what was Martin thinking of?" Christine asked.

Allie sighed. "The two of them were always fighting. They'd break up one week, get back together the next. She always felt insecure around his friends. They were all older. They all had their driver's licences and they'd go to these wild parties and get drunk." Allie scowled. "She kept saying she wanted to get away from him once and for all. But then, her parents would be away, and she'd be lonely ..." Allie's voice trailed off.

"But you were still around," Christine suggested.

Allie shrugged. "Brittany wanted more. She wanted to be popular. She always has. I think it's because her parents have always ignored her. She's just so desperate for someone, anyone, to pay attention to her," Allie shook her head sadly.

Christine felt so thankful that she and her parents weren't like that, at least any more. She wondered what would have happened if her dad had kept climbing the corporate ladder and had continued to be away as much as he had been. Looking back, she wondered if her parents' marriage would have survived too many more years of the kind of stress they were going through. Certainly her family was much happier now. And Christine sensed too that Brittany's accident was bringing the O'Donnells together in the same kind of way.

"Why is it that we can talk about this kind of stuff and Brittany can't?" Christine asked.

"I don't think she knows how," Allie said, honestly. "It's weird because so many times I've been jealous of Brittany. She seems to have everything. She's pretty, popular, smart and has all the money she ever needs and more. But now I realize that she's never really been happy. Not in all the time I've known her."

"Are you?" Christine asked her friend carefully.

Allie stopped for a moment. "Yeah, you know, I think I am, or at least I'm getting there," she said, as if she was discovering something for the first time. "I was miserable when we first got to North Park. I thought I'd never fit in. Brittany kept running off with the older kids like Martin and dumping me. But now that I'm on the basketball team, I've got my own friends. And my parents and I are getting along better too. They're talking about buying a summer place back in Peterborough, and maybe even moving there someday."

Christine was relieved to hear Allie's answer. But she wished there was something they could do to help Brittany.

"It's so strange, you know," Allie added, her voice dropping almost to a whisper, as they rode the elevator back to Brittany's floor at the hospital. "We all thought being at North Park was going to be such a big deal and our lives were going to be so great. But you know what? I was a lot happier before we moved there, when it was just the three of us hanging out together." Allie gave Christine a tentative smile, the first since Christine's arrival.

As they walked silently through the hallway to Brittany's room, Christine thought about what her friend had said. She shook her head as she remembered how miserable she had been when she first moved to Charlottetown. Then North Park High was the only place she wanted to be. Now she realized how wrong she had been.

Chapter Twenty-Eight

RECOVERY

*B*rittany brightened as the girls prepared the display of lighthouses. She directed them from her bed, pointing where she wanted the pictures to go. When they were done, she lay back, gazing at the wall.

"I'm going to lie here and think about your lighthouse," Brittany told Christine. "And your lighthouse keeper. I'd like to meet him this summer, when I get out of this damn hospital."

Allie looked over at Christine and smiled. "Okay, but I'm going to charge you for the tour," Christine teased.

"Deal," Brittany replied. She winced in pain as she moved her leg slightly but seemed contented again to lie back and gaze at the display on her wall.

"I wish you could stay here longer," Allie said to Christine. "This feels like old times. All we need is some ice cream and Diet Coke."

"That's it," Brittany squealed. "Now that would make me feel better."

"What would make you feel better?" All three girls turned as Marilyn Walker appeared in the doorway. "Hi, Christine," she said cheerfully, then turned back to her daughter.

Christine was amazed that Brittany's mom even remembered her name. Over the years, they had only met a handful of times, and usually Marilyn Walker was rushing out the door to some social function. She was tall, like her daughter, and had styled blonde hair. She was in full makeup and was wearing an expensive, tailored navy blue suit. Christine noticed that Brittany's mom had dark circles under her eyes and looked older since the last time she had seen her.

"We were just saying that this felt like old times," Brittany explained coolly to her mother, turning her head away as Marilyn bent over to kiss her cheek. "Usually we'd have chocolate-chocolate chip ice cream and Diet Coke."

"Well, I'll just have to round some up then," Marilyn replied, pulling out her cell phone before Brittany could answer.

"Excuse me, ma'am," said a nurse, who happened to be walking past the doorway. "You're not allowed to use your cell phone in the hospital."

"Mom, you could knock out someone's pacemaker," Brittany said, disparagingly. Marilyn snapped her phone shut. "I'll be right back," she said, bustling out of the door. Christine stared after her, puzzled, and then turned to Brittany with raised eyebrows.

"Oh, they're rising to the occasion," Brittany answered her friend's inquiring look. "Nothing like a challenge to bring out the best in Marilyn and Doug Walker."

"Your mom and dad have been really worried about you," Allie said in their defence.

"Oh, don't worry. They'll disappear again as soon as I get better," Brittany replied bitterly. "After all, those big sales can wait only so long. I'm sure they still manage to fit in a few house

184

showings between visits to the hospital — although I'm sure they don't mention that they have a daughter who's crippled now."

Brittany turned her head away from her friends and was startled to see her mother standing in the doorway. The smile had vanished from Marilyn Walker's face and she leaned against the door frame, as if she needed to hold herself up. She stared at her daughter with eyes filled with anger and hurt. Allie and Christine exchanged uncomfortable looks.

"Can you girls excuse us for a few minutes?" Brittany's mom said. Allie and Christine started moving to the door, but Brittany waved for them to stop.

"Whatever you have to say to me, you can say it in front of my best friends," she said, in an imperious tone. Marilyn looked at the girls. Bright, red spots appeared on her cheeks and she flipped her phone open and closed, in a nervous rhythm.

"I know I've been a terrible parent, Brittany, but we've got to get over that now," Brittany's mom murmured. "All that matters is that you get better."

"But I'm never going to 'get better,' Mother," Brittany snapped. "And if you and dad had been around more, maybe I wouldn't be such a screw-up."

"You're right. We should have been around more," Marilyn replied, her voice rising in intensity. She seemed to forget the other two girls in the room and focused all her energy on willing her daughter to listen. Christine and Allie exchanged uncomfortable glances.

"I don't know how this happened," Brittany's mother continued. "I never meant to be a bad parent. Neither did your dad. You just never seemed to need us."

"How would you know? You were never there. Francesca was the only one around our house," Brittany answered her mother defiantly. "Selling houses and making money and

185

running in the right circles. That's all that mattered to you. I don't know why you had me in the first place."

Allie and Christine were getting more and more uneasy. They looked pleadingly at Brittany, trying to edge towards the door. "Stay where you are," their friend commanded.

"Brittany," Marilyn said tenderly, holding her daughter's hand in her own. Though she was shaking with anger, Brittany didn't try to take her hand away. "You are the best thing that ever happened to me," Marilyn whispered. "It took this horrible accident to make me realize that."

Brittany's eyes welled up with tears. Her mother passed her a Kleenex, and Brittany leaned forward, falling into her mother's open arms. Allie and Christine quickly slipped out the door.

Neither of them spoke as they rode the elevator down to the lobby and made their way back to the O'Donnell's car.

"How's she doing?" Mrs. O'Donnell asked the girls as they climbed in.

"Better," Allie replied. "Her mom was there." She didn't say anything else but Christine knew that her friend was as upset as she was. They didn't get a chance to talk about the scene in Brittany's room until later that night as they got ready for bed in Allie's room.

"What was that all about? With Brittany's mom at the hospital?" Christine asked Allie.

"I don't know," Allie answered. "What do you think?"

Christine shook her head. "They've never been able to get along, in all the time I've known Brittany. Her mom was always too busy. Brittany said that all her mom cared about was real estate. And Brittany always seemed kind of jealous when she would see my mom and I spend time together."

"Do you really think things can change now?" Allie wondered out loud.

"Sure," Christine answered. "Look at us. We've both changed since last year, haven't we?"

The next morning at the hospital, the girls almost bumped into Marilyn Walker coming out of Brittany's room. She gave them a weak smile. "Francesca has brought over some ice cream and Diet Coke as requested," she said, her voice still shaky with emotion. "Brittany is waiting to see you."

Just before they went into Brittany's room, Marilyn gave each of them a hug. Christine was so shocked, she was almost limp as Marilyn hugged her. "I want to thank both of you for being such good friends," Marilyn said softly. "You've meant a lot to Brittany over the years. And I'm sorry I didn't get to know you better, Christine. And Allie. From what Brittany tells me, you're both definitely worth knowing." And with that, she swept away down the hallway. Christine saw Marilyn brush away a few tears as she stood waiting for the elevator.

The girls took a deep breath and entered Brittany's room. She was sitting up in bed, brightly chatting away with Francesca. The older woman fluttered around Brittany, tucking in the covers and gently fixing the girl's hair. Brittany waved a pair of spoons at Christine and Allie and patted the bed.

"Dig in," she urged them. "Thanks, Francesca. As usual, you are the best."

Francesca bent over and kissed Brittany on the forehead before she rushed out the door, overcome with emotion.

The girls were soon happily digging out spoonfuls of ice cream. "Don't worry. There are a couple more containers down at the nurse's station." Brittany giggled.

After a few spoonfuls of ice cream, Brittany put her spoon down and looked from one friend to the other. She looked as if she was about to cry again. "So, guess what my mom told me?" she said. "She's quitting the real estate business. She says it's time for her to slow down and spend more time doing things she really cares about. I'm not sure what that means, because my mother has never done anything but sell real estate. But I guess it's good."

"And your dad?" Allie asked.

"Well, apparently he and my mom have been in marriage counselling, if you can believe it. It was nice of them to let me know. But my mom insists that things are going better now," Brittany explained, dropping yet another bombshell on her friends.

Christine was amazed that her friend was so calm about the news. Maybe she suspected something all along, Christine thought to herself.

"They want to sell the house, move to something more homey. And we're going to Europe, as soon as my leg is better. All three of us, can you believe it? We've never gone on a holiday together."

"That's great news, Brittany," Christine said, and Allie nodded her agreement, passing the ice cream back in Brittany's direction.

After they finished eating, Allie gave Brittany a hug. "I'll be back later. Chrissie, we'll be waiting downstairs. We should leave for the airport soon."

As she sat on the bed beside Brittany, Christine realized that she no longer felt the dread that she had experienced the day before. Brittany was going to be okay. It was just going to take some time.

"I can't wait to come out and visit you," Brittany said, glancing over at the collection of lighthouse pictures on the wall. Then a frown appeared on her face. "I didn't tell you the truth about my parents," she said, her voice dropping to a whisper. Christine waited for her friend to continue. "This is our first and last family trip together," Brittany explained, a tone of bitterness creeping into her voice. "How's that for irony? My mom is putting up a brave front but I'm pretty sure they're going to split up."

"How do you feel?" Christine asked softly, examining her friend's bandaged face for clues.

Brittany shrugged. "It's been one helluva week. My life has certainly changed."

"Mine too," Christine said.

"What do you mean?" Brittany asked.

"I think my family was going in the same direction," Christine explained. "If we had stayed in Toronto, and my dad kept working so much ... who knows? Maybe my parents would have split up too."

"Why do they do that?" Brittany inquired, her voice shaking slightly. "First they make me miserable. Then they make me more miserable." She giggled at her own observation. "I can't believe I'm pissed off at them for splitting up. I mean, it's not as if we were your average nuclear family to begin with."

"Yeah, but that doesn't make it hurt any less," Christine answered, shaking her head. "I'm glad that you and your mom are getting along better now."

"You know, I always wanted us to be like you and your mom," Brittany confessed suddenly. "I was always so jealous. You two got along so well. She did stuff with you and she always seemed to be there when you needed her."

"Oh, we still had our fights," Christine corrected her friend. "But you're right. I am lucky. I guess I never really realized it before now." There was a moment of silence as the two girls looked out the window.

"You can call me any time," Christine said finally, getting up and giving Brittany a quick hug. "We can talk about this stuff now."

"I wish you were still here, Chrissie," Brittany's eyes were welling up with tears. "But I'm glad you're happy."

As Christine left the room, she turned back and saw Brittany staring contentedly at the collection of lighthouse photos on the wall.

When they got to the airport, Christine thanked the O'Donnells and gave Allie a big hug.

"Call me every day," Christine whispered. "And keep an eye on her."

"I will," Allie replied tearfully.

As she waited at the gate for her flight to be called, Christine went to a payphone and dialled her home number. She was relieved when her mother answered.

"How's Brittany doing?" Monica asked.

"Much better," Christine reassured her mother. "But the strangest thing happened today." She described the scene between Brittany and her mother. She heard Monica catch her breath when she told her about the Walkers going for counseling. When Christine finished, there was a slight pause.

"How does Brittany feel about all of this? It must be a bit of a shock to her after everything she's been through," Monica said sympathetically.

"She was hurt and angry, but now I think she's relieved," Christine answered honestly. "She's been so unhappy for years. It's just too bad that she and her mother couldn't have worked things out sooner."

"I'm glad that you and I were never like that. Or were we? I guess we were heading in that direction, too, for a while there."

"No, we were never like that. I mean, I didn't understand what Dad was going through with his job. And I was mad about moving to Charlottetown. But I never felt as though you guys had forgotten about me."

There was another short pause as mother and daughter thought about everything their family had been through over the last seven months. "So we'll see you in a couple of hours," Monica said finally.

"Yep," Christine replied. "I love you, Mom," she added, just before she hung up the phone.

"I love you, too, Chrissie," her mother answered.

As she sat on the airplane waiting for take-off, Christine thought about her friendship with Brittany. There was a bond between the girls that would last, no matter how far apart they were. Brittany still had a long way to go in her recovery, both in body and mind. But Christine sensed that the accident had been a turning point for all of the Walkers.

As the plane lifted off from Pearson and started to wing its way east, Christine began to think about the problems that awaited her back on the Island. She was worried how Mack was going to react when he found out that the lighthouse was being turned into a cottage development. And then there was her argument with Scott. What did he mean when he said there was something he wanted to talk about? Christine's heart sank. All of a sudden, she wasn't in a rush to get back to the Island after all.

Chapter Twenty-Nine

SCOTT'S FUTURE

*T*he next day, after school, Scott and Christine sat on a bench in the Confederation Landing park, eating their ice cream cones from Cows, the ice cream store that had become one of the favourite hangouts for Christine and her friends. She and Scott watched the powerboats and sailboats heading in and out of the marina. Christine thought about their first date on the CHRISTOPHER ROBIN. The boat was now moored about forty-five minutes from Charlottetown, at a tiny harbour near Pinette, just off the main highway. She frowned as she thought about how angry Scott had been with her before she left for Toronto. The romance aboard the CHRISTO-PHER ROBIN now seemed a long time ago.

Scott had been cryptic when Christine asked him what he had been up to while she was away. She could tell that something was bothering him but she wasn't sure what it was. He looked as if he wanted to say something to her but he insisted that she tell him about her trip first.

"It was so awful to see her bandaged up like that. And her leg …"Christine's voice trailed off.

Scott listened attentively as Christine told him about Brittany's confrontation and reconciliation with her mother.

"It was tough seeing Brittany and her mom argue like that. But I get the feeling that everything's going to work out for them now," Christine finished.

"I wish I could say the same."

Christine's heart dropped. It was the moment she had been dreading. Scott was going to break up with her. She stared out at the harbour, willing herself not to start crying.

"I don't know what to do," Scott said. "My dad and Doug insist that I have to come fish with them. Remember when Dad hurt his back stacking those traps? Well, now he can't haul the gear right. If I help, all the money stays in family. Otherwise, Dad has to hire someone and that would cut into the take for the season."

Christine felt a huge sense of relief to find out what was bothering Scott. The words and anger came tumbling out of him as if he had been storing them up, waiting for her to get back.

"I won't do it," he said stubbornly. "I can't do it."

"Why not?" Christine asked. She liked Scott's dad and she sensed that he was really counting on Scott to help. Mr. MacFarlane was older than her own father, and his face was etched with deep lines from many years of exposure to the wind and saltwater.

"I don't want to become a fisherman," Scott replied, tossing his napkin into the nearby garbage can. "If I do this now, they'll think that I've changed my mind. It will be all the same arguments, all the same pressure. It's not only the money. I think it's their way of pushing me into the business."

Christine was surprised. Scott had never told her that this was an ongoing debate in the MacFarlane family. She knew that Scott wanted to study computer science and was hoping to get a hockey scholarship to Acadia University when they were finished high school. She assumed that his family supported that decision, but maybe not.

"What's wrong with fishing?" Christine asked. "Jennifer's dad fished for lobster. I hear you can make a good living."

Scott gave her a scowl. "That's easy for you to say," he said. "You've never been out on a lobster boat. It's hard work under lousy conditions. You never know what price you're going to get. That's all controlled by people from away. And yes, you can make a good living — if there are any lobsters left to catch."

Christine was surprised at the bitterness of Scott's tone. He continued, in an angry voice. "You know, you think it's so glamorous, this life by the sea," he snapped. "Well, it's not. My grandfather lost his boat in a storm and the family had to live on welfare for years. My father's brother hit the bottle after a couple of bad seasons and he lost his boat to the bank. My dad's back is shot, thanks to years of hard labour. And now my brother wants to throw his life away, too. Isn't that a lovely picture of life on the Island?"

Scott got up abruptly and walked down towards the water. Christine watched as he picked up a few stones and tried to make them skip across the surface of the harbour. Finally he turned back to the bench and returned to where Christine was still sitting.

"I'm sorry," he said, quietly. "I didn't mean to take it out on you. I just don't want to do it."

"You'll have to tell your father then."

"But he won't listen."

"Just talk to him."

Scott shrugged his shoulders, then nodded. "I'll try."

Christine decided to change the subject. "How's Mack doing?"

Scott shook his head. "He still can't talk or walk. But he gets outside some now. Sits and looks across at the lighthouse."

"I need to go see them. I miss them."

Scott smiled. "Why don't you go now? I have to head home and help out with some chores."

He gave her a kiss and jogged off towards home. Christine watched him disappear, happy that he had been willing to confide in her. She turned in the opposite direction and followed the boardwalk past the hotel where she and her parents stayed when they first arrived in Charlottetown. She continued along the boardwalk to a large apartment complex, right on the water.

As promised, the McIntosh apartment looked out over the harbour, towards the Governors Light in the distance. It was a sunny afternoon, and after a warm greeting, Betty helped Christine roll Mack's wheelchair onto a tiny balcony outside the McIntosh apartment. Mack had on a heavy sweater, with a wool blanket over his knees. He was still frail but the fresh air over the last couple of weeks had brought back some colour to his face. He had a chalkboard resting on his lap and he clutched a piece of chalk in his good hand. This was how he communicated now. It was slow work for him to get his message across so most of the time he and Christine just sat and watched the boats in the harbour and stared at the tiny flash of the lighthouse in the distance.

Christine thought back to her first time at the top of lighthouse and the magical feelings that had followed. She looked sadly over at the old lightkeeper.

"I told him, dear," Betty said when Christine went inside to get another blanket for Mack. "About the cottages. I hope you don't mind. I just didn't want to hold back the good news."

Christine frowned. She forgot that she had asked them not to tell Mack.

"The good news?"

"Yes, dear. We're so thankful that the lighthouse will be saved."

Christine wanted to argue but she didn't want to seem disrespectful. Everyone, it seemed, was in favour of the cottages being built, even if they were turning the lighthouse into another tourist trap. She wished that she could talk to Mack about it, but trying to communicate with the old man was a painstaking process. She didn't want to upset him by telling him that she thought the cottages were a bad idea.

Christine went back out onto the balcony. As she sat with Mack, Christine thought about Scott's problems with his family. She wondered what Mack would think of Scott's decision to give up fishing. Mack's family also chose to go away, to Alberta, and to leave the Island and the lighthouses behind. It's like the end of an era, she thought sadly, more of the brain drain that Jennifer had told her about. At the same time, she could see the young people's point of view. They had a chance for a better living and they weren't taking their life in their own hands every time they went to work.

"Mack," Christine said quietly, "Jennifer's dad told us the story about the Old Salt's brother and his nephews. Did they really die on Malpeque Bay?"

The old lightkeeper nodded sadly. He looked as if he wanted to tell her more but couldn't.

"If it were me, I don't think I'd like the ocean anymore," Christine continued. "And all those stories he tells us, about the shipwrecks and all the people who have died. It's so dangerous."

Mack shrugged and looked out again at the water. Suddenly, he took the chalk in his hand and carefully began to write on the board that rested on his lap. Christine waited eagerly to see what he had written. Finally, he handed the board to her.

"Live by the sea," she read off the board. "Die by the sea." And Mack took his good hand and tapped himself on the heart.

Christine was silent. She nodded to him, gratefully.

Betty came bustling out of the apartment laden with a tray of tea and sweets. She helped Mack grip a mug of tea in his good hand and laid out a few cookies and fudge within his reach. She pulled a chair over beside Christine and her husband, and her gaze too turned towards the lighthouse.

Mack turned to his wife and gestured with his head in Christine's direction. Betty looked at him quizzically, then realized what he was trying to ask her.

"Mack and I were talking the other day. We realized that we had never heard how you and Jennifer did on your project," Betty explained.

Christine looked at her blankly. Then she smiled. "Oh, you mean the lighthouse project," she exclaimed. She had forgotten that her friendship with the old couple had started with the project for Social Studies.

Mack gave his head a vigorous nod.

"An A+." Christine smiled. Mack nodded his head and grinned his approval.

As they sat looking out across the harbour, a cloud came over Christine's face as she thought about the lighthouse project. She wasn't sure that she really deserved the mark, or the appreciation of the McIntoshes. After all, the idea had been that they could stay in the lighthouse. That hadn't happened. And the heritage committee wasn't able to get enough money to set up the lighthouse display, either. Mack didn't know that the tool shed had been torn down, and that all his lighthouse memorabilia was now collecting dust in an old potato warehouse. Christine felt as though she had let the old couple down, but she didn't have the heart to tell them. Looking at the weathered profile of the old man sitting next to her, Christine gently picked up Mack's hand. "I'm sorry," she whispered into the wind.

Chapter Thirty

RETURN TO
THE LIGHTHOUSE

*I*n June, Christine's father announced that his company was holding a business meeting out at the Governors Lighthouse.

"We've booked the entire place for the weekend," Rob explained. "We've got buyers coming in from across North America and we wanted somewhere special to put them up. Luckily for us, Danny Redmond had the cottages ready a week ahead of schedule."

Christine didn't look impressed. Her father noticed her expression.

"Why don't the two of you come out and take a look sometime over the weekend?" he suggested to Christine and her mom. "Bring Scott and Jennifer along if you like."

"I don't think so," Christine muttered, getting up from the table.

"She's still so disappointed," her mother said, as Christine left the room.

"I don't understand why. The McIntoshes couldn't have stayed there. I thought she'd be pleased that the Old Salt got to stay at least," he added loudly, hoping his daughter was within hearing.

"What?" Christine said, coming back into the kitchen. "The Old Salt is still there?"

Her dad gave her a pleased look. "It was your mother's idea. She suggested that the place needed a night watchman. She convinced Mr. Redmond to hire the Old Salt. After all, he knows the place inside out."

Christine smiled at her mom. "That's really cool."

"Remember, the offer stands. We'll be there all weekend," her dad told her.

When Jennifer and Scott heard about the Old Salt, they were both eager to go out and visit the old sailor. Monica agreed to take them out Sunday morning.

"Do you have to go out on the boat?" she asked Scott, who was sitting in the kitchen, munching on a sandwich.

He shook his head morosely. Scott had finally agreed to help his brother fish a couple of mornings a week, even though it meant missing some school. He was constantly complaining about the early hours and hard work.

"We only get Sunday off," he grumbled. "My brother actually wants me to skip school next week to help out. I tried to explain that we're getting close to exams but he just won't listen. All he cares about is making as much money as possible. My marks don't seem to matter."

"Have you explained that to your father?" Monica said, trying to help.

Scott shook his head. "If I say anything to my father, he just says I'm lazy. And I'm not. I just don't want to fish. I want to go to university."

"What about one of the teachers? Could they speak to your dad?" Christine suggested.

Again Scott shook his head. "They're just a bunch of folks from town. No offence." He munched his sandwich in silence, as the Millers exchanged worried looks.

The next day Monica and Christine picked up Jennifer and Scott and drove to the Governors Lighthouse. As they reached the end of the paved road, they saw a big wooden sign that read, "The Governors Light Cottages." Christine was happy to see that the sign was not too gaudy. She strained to see the cottages in the woods. Her mother noticed her surprise.

"That was one of the conditions," her mother explained, with a pleased expression on her face. "He couldn't just rip down the woods. The environment had to remain as natural as possible. And the cottages are all built of wood, to blend in with the forest."

When they finally passed through the trees and the light-house appeared, Christine caught her breath. The Governors Light had been painted, and the red and white stripes gleamed in the summer sun. The lighthouse was as beautiful as ever.

There were cars scattered around the wooden cottages, and a main reception building had been built where the old tool shed was. It was the same design as the old building, and was also painted a bright white with red trim.

"That's where your father's group is meeting," Christine's mom explained. "But we'll go right into the lighthouse. The Old Salt should be expecting us."

As if on cue, the old sailor came walking up a path from the cottages.

"G'day to you all," he said with a jaunty wave.

"How's it going?" Scott asked, shaking hands with the old man. They all followed him up the stairs into the lighthouse.

The place was almost empty. Christine looked sadly around the room which still reminded her so much of the McIntoshes. Most of their furniture had been moved across the harbour, and all their pictures and mementoes were gone. Only a few chairs and tables remained. There was an old cot over on one side of the room near the woodstove. The room seemed lonely, a shadow of itself.

"It's busy here, now," the old man began, pointing to the chairs. He motioned for the visitors to gather around the woodstove. He settled into a big armchair. Christine recognized his favourite chair when he used to visit Betty and Mack. They had decided to leave it for him, she thought sadly.

"I've got lots to do, keeping an eye on the place. And Marco Polo will scare any prowlers away," the old man added, a twinkle in his eye. The teenagers stifled a giggle, looking down at the tiny, good-natured dog. As if on cue, Marco Polo slumped to the ground, his eyes closing as he rested his head on the toe of the Old Salt's rubber boot. Everyone laughed.

"Does anyone come in here?" Jennifer asked, looking around the dusty lighthouse building.

"No," the old sailor said, shaking his head sadly. "They won't have tours or nothing. For insurance reasons. I'm just lucky they let me stay here at all." He gave Monica a grateful grin. "But Betty and Mack feel better knowing I'm here, in charge of the operation."

Again Christine felt a wave of disappointment. The idea had been to preserve the lighthouse as a heritage site. Now no one was going to experience the magic of the light. She was sure everyone else in the room shared her disappointment, especially her mom. She had worked hard to make sure the Old Salt could stay at the lighthouse. Obviously the new owners weren't too interested in sharing the history of the old light.

"We might as well have a story while we're at 'er," the Old Salt suggested and the group pulled their chairs into a circle around the old man. Christine felt like a kid at summer camp, gathering around the bonfire to tell ghost stories. She noticed that everyone waited eagerly for the Old Salt to begin.

"The year was 1851, October. More than one hundred schooners, all sails set, were headed to the mackerel grounds off the north shore. The fishermen had come from Nova Scotia and New England, hopin' to take away a load o' mackerel," the Old Salt began. Christine closed her eyes and imagined the sight of the old, mighty ships. One hundred of them, she thought, awestruck at the picture the Old Salt conjured up in her mind.

"It was late in the season and so many of the captains kept an anxious watch. Sure enough, the wind started blowin' late in the day and a heavy swell rose." The old man paused, and patted Marco Polo on the head.

"The next mornin', the waters were a fury of foam and crashin' waves. The wind shifted east, then nort' and the storm continued all day Saturday, all day Sunday." He shook his head sadly. "From Nort' Cape to East Point, the beaches were littered with debris. The destruction was almost too much for the eye to take in. On the Cavendish shore, thirteen men hung from the rigging. They had lashed themselves to the ship, hopin' to survive the fearful wrath." The Old Salt's eyes glistened with moisture. Watching him, Christine was reminded of his own loss, of the brother and nephews who were also swallowed up by the sea.

"From the eastern shores to the North Cape, they figgered there were more than eighty wrecks. One hundred and fifty sailors. More lost at sea." He paused again, and taking a yellowed handkerchief from his pocket, he wiped his eyes. "One captain from New England lost four sons and a nephew. From PE Island to Boston, the Yankee Gale is forever remembered as one of the most tragic storms we ever seen in these parts."

The Old Salt concluded his story and leaned back in his armchair. Christine noticed that Scott was staring out the window of the lighthouse at the now peaceful waters of the Charlottetown Harbour. They were so beautiful now, she thought, and yet, they could also be so deadly. She shuddered and pulled her sweater closer around her.

"Enough of the gloom," the Old Salt said, pulling his guitar out. He burst into a rousing chorus of his favourite sea chantey. Scott and Jennifer joined in while Monica and Christine clapped along and stamped their feet in time to the music.

Come cheer up my lads, it's to glory we steer
To add something more to this wonderful year
To honor we call you, as free men, not slaves
For who are so free as the sons of the waves

Heart of oak are our ships
Heart of oak are our men
We always are ready
Steady, boys, steady
We'll fight and we'll conquer, again and again

Our worthy forefathers, let's give them a cheer
To climates unknown did courageously steer
Through oceans to deserts, for freedom they came
And dying, bequeathed us their freedom and fame.

As they headed towards the Jeep, the Old Salt and Marco Polo waved to them from the front step.

"He just suits the place, doesn't he?" Monica said as they got settled in the Jeep.

"I'm sure Mack and Betty will be happy to know that their home is in good hands," Jennifer agreed.

A group of people in sweaters and jeans came pouring out of the main reception room. Rob Miller broke away from them to walk over to the Jeep.

"So, what do you think?" he asked with a grin.

"It's pretty nice," Christine replied honestly. "But I wish the lighthouse was open, too."

"I know," her father agreed. "Some of the folks from away were asking for tours. But Danny Redmond said it was impossible. We had some pretty disappointed people."

"Why can't they do tours?" Jennifer piped up from the back seat. "Wasn't that part of the arrangement?"

Monica shook her head. "The insurance would cost more than Mr. Redmond wanted to pay. They had to agree to keep visitors out of the light. Believe me, I tried."

"Well, it looks great from the outside," Scott suggested. "And the Old Salt adds a real touch of the Island, doesn't he?" Everyone laughed. They waved goodbye to Rob Miller and headed back to town.

When they got home, there was a message on the answering machine from Brittany in Toronto. Christine called her friend back.

"Guess what?" Brittany announced. "We're coming to visit you."

"You are? When?" Christine asked, surprised.

"Actually my mom has been talking to your mom and Allie's mom. It's all set. We'll be there for the Canada Day weekend. It's my mom's idea, to celebrate the end of school," Brittany explained.

"How's it going? With your mom?" Christine asked tentatively. Though she talked frequently with Brittany, she wasn't always sure when her friend was telling her everything about how things were going.

"Okay, I guess," Brittany replied. "She's trying really hard. We both are. But I think she finds this full-time mom business a little boring. And she is kind of cramping my style. I'm used to doing everything my way."

Christine smiled. Same old Brittany. "How's the physio?"

Brittany sighed. "It's a lot harder than I thought. I never realized how difficult it is to get around in a wheelchair. It takes so much longer to do anything. And the cane, well, that's really attractive too."

"Brittany, who cares! The important thing is that you're walking."

"If you can call it walking." Brittany paused. "The first thing we have to do is to visit that lighthouse of yours. And I can't wait to meet Scott."

"It'll be like old times," Christine replied. Then, she regretted her words. It wouldn't be like old times, at least not for Brittany.

"I'll call you next week to plan our agenda," Brittany said.

Later that night, Christine was watching TV when her dad returned from his weekend meeting.

"Where's your mom?" he asked, a worried look on his face.

"Right here," Monica said, appearing at the top of the stairs. "Good weekend?"

Rob nodded. "We've got a problem. Actually, you've got a problem."

Monica looked surprised. "What's the problem?"

"It's the Old Salt," he replied.

"Is he okay?" Christine asked anxiously.

"Yes, he's fine," her father reassured her. "But he's too friendly with the guests. At least, that's Danny Redmond's opinion. He wants him to stay away from the guests."

"What do you mean?" Monica asked.

"He keeps walking around visiting the cottages, telling stories to anyone who will listen," Rob explained. "I think it's great. But it's not Danny's idea of what the place is about. He wants the cottages to be upscale, classy. The Old Salt isn't what he's looking for."

"But he belongs there," Christine said, exasperated. "And his stories are wonderful."

The phone rang. "That's probably Danny Redmond now," Rob said to his wife, who went to answer the phone.

She returned ten minutes later, worry written across her face. "He says the Old Salt has to go. He asked him to stop and he wouldn't. He wants him out of the lighthouse before the cottages open next weekend." She sank to the steps. "What am I going to tell that dear old man?" she said sadly.

The next day at school, Jennifer and Scott were appalled to hear the news about the Old Salt.

"Do you think we could have a protest? You know, picket signs and stuff," Jennifer suggested.

"I don't want to embarrass the Old Salt," Christine replied.

"He might enjoy being the centre of attention. He's not exactly a wallflower!" Scott joked.

"Let's meet after school and come up with a plan. Maybe we can write a letter to the editor or something like that?" Christine suggested.

As Jennifer and Christine arrived in Social Studies class, they were surprised to see Melanie waving them over.

"I hear that my dad is kicking that crazy old man out of the lighthouse," she said. "My dad says that he's kind of sorry he got into the deal in the first place. It was my idea, of course." Melanie looked pleased with herself. "I'm sure he'll feel better once he gets rid of the old guy."

Christine started to argue with Melanie, but Jennifer tugged her on the sleeve and pulled her to the back of the class.

"Ignore her," Jennifer whispered. "She's just trying to get some attention. I hear her dad is having money problems. That's probably why he's in such a bad mood."

That night at the supper table, Christine told her parents about what Melanie had said. Her mom and dad looked troubled.

"There's a rumour around that Danny wants to get rid of the cottages," Rob told them. "He has an offer to build a golf course up near Cavendish but his money is all tied up in the development at the lighthouse."

"Maybe that's why he's being so tough on the Old Salt," Monica murmured.

"Don't you see? This is our chance to get the cottages and the lighthouse back," Christine said eagerly.

"It's really not realistic, Chrissie," he said gently. "That's a three hundred thousand dollar investment. I don't know anyone who has that kind of cash just kicking around."

"But what about the Old Salt? He won't have to move if we can find someone else to buy the cottages."

"I'm working on the Old Salt," Monica replied. "Danny has agreed to give him one more chance. I was out at the lighthouse today, talking to him. He doesn't understand what he's done wrong. He's just doing what he does best — talking. I explained it as best I could. The cottages don't open until the weekend. Let's hope Danny has cooled off by then and will just let things be."

"I'm sure that if he was going to sell the cottages, we would have heard by now," Rob added. "It's probably just PEI gossip, nothing to it."

"What time do the girls arrive?" Monica asked, strategically changing the subject.

"Brittany says the first thing she wants to do is to visit the lighthouse," Christine said. Her friends were scheduled to arrive that Friday, just in time for the long weekend.

"Will she be able to make it up there?" Christine's dad asked his wife, who had been talking to Brittany's mother.

"She uses a wheelchair some of the time, and has a cane. It depends how tired she is. Someone will have to carry her up, I guess," Monica said thoughtfully. "That is, if we can convince Danny to let us go up there."

"He has to," Christine said emphatically. "If you tell him her story, he has to let her up there."

"I don't want you to get her hopes up, Chrissie. It may not be possible. Especially with her ... condition," her father replied.

Christine's heart sank. She knew that going to the top of the lighthouse meant everything to Brittany. She didn't want to disappoint her friend. She had to find a way.

Chapter Thirty-One

ON THE BOARDWALK

School ended on Friday morning, and as she said goodbye to her teachers at Queen Charlotte, Christine was amazed at how much she was going to miss the school. Next year she and her friends would move to Colonel Gray High School, just across the field from the junior high. Christine wasn't looking forward to changing schools again, but this time, at least, she was not going to be the new girl in town.

As she stood at the airport waiting for the girls to arrive, she felt strangely nervous as she watched the small plane taxi up to the gate. Although she had talked to her friends on the phone, this was the first time she would see Brittany since she got out of the hospital. Christine knew that Brittany used a cane to support herself when she walked and she was also bringing a wheelchair, to use when she got tired.

Christine wasn't quite sure what to expect as she watched the flight attendant helping Brittany down the stairs. As her friends got closer, Christine started to wave. She rushed to the sliding doors and threw her arms around Brittany, who grinned up at her from a wheelchair. "I'm so glad you're here," Christine said, carefully letting go of Brittany and turning to give Allie a hug.

"Almost as good as new," Brittany said wryly. Her bandages were all gone and there were only a few tiny scars left over from the plastic surgery. Her face was tanned her family's trip to Europe. She had sent Christine postcards from the south of France, Italy and Greece.

Allie too beamed from one friend to another.

"You look great," she whispered to Christine.

"You too," Christine replied. Allie looked happier than the last time Christine had seen her in Toronto. She wore a tee-shirt with the North Park team logo, shorts and running shoes. Her hair was brown now, her original colour, with no more of the blonde highlights that she had put in at Brittany's suggestion a couple of years ago. Allie wore hardly any makeup and she seemed taller and more athletic than ever. Christine was thrilled to see Allie looking so relaxed and confident.

The three girls giggled their way through supper at a local steakhouse, while Rob and Monica looked on, bemused. Later, they sat on the Miller's porch, having their traditional feast of chocolate-chocolate chip ice cream. This time, though, it was the local ice cream from Cows, which Christine proudly served to her friends.

"You've turned into quite the supporter of Island culture," Brittany teased her. "But you've got some excellent motivation, don't you? And speaking of which, when do we get to meet this romantic Islander of yours?"

Christine felt her face turning a shade of red that made her friends laugh even harder. "Tomorrow night," she mumbled. "We've got a special tour planned."

"To the lighthouse?" Brittany asked. She had been pestering Christine since she arrived for a trip out to the light. Christine nodded.

"Why can't we go tonight?" Brittany pleaded.

"Maybe we'll head down to the harbour and look at it from this side," Christine suggested. "But they're planning something for tomorrow night. And they won't even tell me what it is."

"Who are they?" Allie asked, intrigued.

"Scott and Jennifer and my parents," Christine replied. She had been so busy getting ready for her friends' visit that she hadn't really had time to think about the so-called surprise. Now her curiosity was piqued. What could they have planned?

Her parents hadn't said anything more about the Old Salt. Christine assumed that meant that the old man was allowed to stay at the cottages. She wasn't sure if they had also been able to convince Danny Redmond to allow them to go up the lighthouse. She hoped so.

"It's getting dark now, Chrissie," Brittany piped in. "Let's go see this famous light."

Christine frowned. She looked over at her friend, not quite sure how they could get down to the boardwalk. Brittany followed Christine's gaze to the wheelchair, folded up on one side of the porch.

"Allie, can you get the chair set up?" Brittany asked, taking matters in her own hands, giving Christine a reassuring smile. "If you help me down the stairs, we'll get rolling."

Brittany soon had the girls laughing with her clumsy efforts to steer herself over the bumpy sidewalks along North River Road. But she insisted on doing it herself.

"I've been a spoiled brat all my life." She grinned. "It's time for me to stand on my own two feet. Ha. Get it."

Allie winced slightly but Brittany laughed, and eventually all three girls had a bad case of the giggles. Soon they reached Victoria Park, and made their way past the ball diamonds to the road leading down to the boardwalk. Christine felt bad every time Brittany hit a rut or a broken piece of pavement. She admired her friend's desire to be independent. Same old stubborn Brittany, she thought with a smile.

The girls waited for their turn to cross the busy road that went through Victoria Park. It was a glorious summer evening. There was a steady stream of cars, filled with families and young couples out for a drive. The ice cream shop was doing a booming business, and competing waves of rock music drifted from the cars parked along the boardwalk. High atop the hillside, the old cannons stood guard, while the Canadian flag fluttered in the evening breeze.

When they reached the boardwalk, Brittany waved for the girls to stop. She took a deep breath, slowly gazing from one end of the harbour to the other.

"I wouldn't take a deep breath like that at low tide," Christine giggled. Her friends turned to her puzzled. "The water's clean," Christine explained, "but it stinks like rotting seaweed."

"How can you tell what tide it is now?" Allie asked.

"Well, it's pretty high now," she pointed to the shoreline. "See how those rocks are almost all covered. If we come back at low tide, the water will be out far enough that we see some of the sandy bottom."

"That's really cool," Allie replied.

"I see it," Brittany squealed suddenly. She pointed way out across the water at the Governors Light flickering in the distance.

"Wait until the sun goes down," Christine promised.

"Where's the best place to see it?" Brittany asked urgently.

Christine glanced up at the cannons but realized that climbing the hill was out of the question. "Why don't we head down that way?" Christine suggested, pointing to a bench farther along the boardwalk.

"What about up there?" Brittany said stubbornly. "If you two help me balance, I can make it up there."

"I don't know, Brittany, it's awfully steep," Allie tried to change her friend's mind.

Before her friends could protest, Brittany was out of the wheelchair. She grabbed the cane on the back of the chair and started hobbling towards the path leading up the hill. Allie rolled her eyes at Christine and the two of them rushed to help her.

It took several minutes, and by the time they reached the top, Brittany's face was flushed from the exertion. Finally she reached the pinnacle of the hill and she flopped to the grass, next to the cannons. "I'll be faster going down," she joked, trying to catch her breath. Looking out at the harbour again, Brittany gasped with pleasure. The sun had dipped below the horizon, but the afterglow had spread across the sky. The red Island soil glowed in the fading light, and the sky had turned a deep, velvety shade of blue. Even the grass seemed more alive than usual, turning the most lush green that Christine had ever seen it. All the colours, it seemed, were putting on a show for her visitors from Ontario.

Christine thought about the first time she had sat here, high above the harbour. She was so miserable then, not wanting to stay one more hour on the Island. Beside her, her friends were lost in their own reverie. Like a magnet, the lighthouse had drawn their eyes towards its magical light. Christine wondered if their heartbeats, too, had slowed to beat in time with the mighty beacon.

The girls sat in silence until total darkness fell. Below them, many of the parked cars were driving away, their music fading into the distance. There were still a few stragglers making their way along the boardwalk but most of the families were gone. The ice cream shop was pulling its shutters closed for the evening, and the lights of the tennis courts suddenly went black.

"We'd better head back." Christine's voice sounded strange after such an extended period of silence. Her friends nodded, still not completely back in the real world. As they slowly made their way back through the park, Christine felt a thrill of pleasure. She sensed that her friends had experienced the same mysterious feeling from the lighthouse that she too had felt almost a year ago.

That night, the girls settled into Christine's room. The window was open, and the curtains fluttered slightly in the breeze coming up from the harbour. Brittany was in Christine's bed. Christine and Allie slept on air mattresses and sleeping bags on the floor.

"You're so lucky, Chrissie. This place is beautiful," Allie said, as the girls laid in the darkness.

"Wait until you see the rest of the Island," Christine replied, with a surge of pride. "You ain't seen nothing yet." She fell silent for a moment, as she reflected with surprise at how much she had come to love the Island. "I can't believe how much I hated it here," Christine confessed sheepishly to her friends. "All I wanted was North Park High. That's all that mattered."

"A lot has changed since last summer," Brittany piped in. "Look at my family. My mom and dad are going to split up, as I suspected all along," she continued, her voice dropping almost to a whisper. "We had a good time in Europe, my mom and I. But my dad never really seemed into it. I think he tried, but it just didn't work."

"I'm sorry, Brittany," Christine said thoughtfully. "It's for the best, really," Brittany replied cheerfully. "I guess my dad has been seeing someone else for a couple of years."

Christine was happy that the dark room hid her surprise. She wondered if Allie was as shocked as she was.

"You're okay with that?" Allie asked, sounding concerned.

214

"Sure," Brittany answered. "My mom is talking about moving to Vancouver. And she has to go back to work. But she says she'll stick around Toronto if I want to."

All three girls were quiet for a minute. Then it was Allie's turn.

"My mom and dad want to go back to Peterborough," Allie said slowly, as if she had to force herself say the words out loud. "For good. Like, live there all the time."

"When?" Brittany gasped.

"I don't know," Allie shrugged. "When they went to look for a summer place, they found a year-round house that they totally love. My dad ran into an old friend from law school. They got talking ... and now, they're seriously thinking about moving there."

"I don't believe this," Brittany said, shaking her head. "Last year, it looked like our lives were set. Now look at us."

"It's not so bad," Allie told her friend. "I don't mind. And you know what? I don't think it matters where we all go. Christine moved all the way out here and we're still friends, right?"

"Allie's right," Brittany concluded. "We'll be fine, no matter where we go."

Chapter Thirty-Two

TO THE LIGHTHOUSE

*T*he girls had a whirlwind tour of the Island, despite sleeping in the next day. They picked up bagels and coffee at the Tim Hortons drive-thru — "a PEI tradition" Christine explained to them. Originally, Rob Miller was supposed to go with them but he had a phone call that morning. His boss had called him in to work on the Saturday of the holiday weekend. Christine noticed that her dad seemed tense as he packed up to drive out to the plant.

Her mother seemed distracted, too, as if the phone call from the potato plant had caught her off-guard as well. But Monica Miller shook off her gloom as she headed the car up Brackley Point Road to the Covehead lighthouse. It was a small, sturdy white frame set right on the dunes. On top, a light flashed brightly, even in the brilliant late morning sunshine. Some windsurfers skimmed across the waves just off shore.

"It gets really stormy up here during the winter," Monica explained to the girls. "We saw some pictures on the news of these giant waves rolling in from the north, pounding up here on the beach. This light can come in handy."

"How many lighthouses are there in total?" Allie asked.

"Fourteen," Christine piped in. "They go right from one tip of the Island to the other. You can even get a special certificate if you visit them all."

"Could we do that?" Brittany asked. "It's not that far a drive is it?" She looked at the map on her lap, tracing a route from one end of the island shape to the other.

Monica laughed. "It's a lot farther than it looks," she cautioned. "It takes two hours to get to the eastern tip from Charlottetown. And then it takes another two from town to get to North Cape, which is the farthest point on the western end of the Island. It would be like driving from Toronto to Ottawa."

"Well, we'll have to do it next time, then," Brittany insisted. The three girls piled out of the car and lined up in front of the Covehead light. Monica snapped their picture and the girls stood for a moment, staring out across the waters of the north shore.

Their next stop was another tiny lighthouse, this time in North Rustico. The North Rustico light was also painted a bright red and white and it was now run as a tourist attraction by the relatives of the original lightkeepers. They were greeted at the door by a big man with a booming voice and bushy white whiskers.

"Welcome to Nort' Rustico," he said in a cheery voice. "I'm Bud Gallant. Feel free to take a look through our lighthouse. Take as many photos as you want. If you've got a mind to go out fishin', this is the place to go. Let me know and I can book youse for a tour."

It only took a few minutes for the girls to wander through the four tiny rooms of the lighthouse. Brittany kept muttering the word "tour" over and over again under her breath.

"What are you doing?" Christine asked with a puzzled grin. She and Allie were on either side of Brittany helping her balance. Brittany had insisted on leaving her cane in the car. Their progress was slow, but determined.

"I'm trying to say 'toe-er', the way he said it," Brittany explained. "Hey, he said his name was Gallant. Isn't that the last name of your friend Jennifer? Do you think they're related?"

Christine couldn't help laughing. "Britt, everyone in North Rustico is named Gallant," Christine said through her giggles. "I exaggerate only slightly. Jennifer showed me in the phone book one time. There are two columns of Gallants in the phone book listings for Rustico."

Brittany shook her head. "I don't know how you keep track of all of this stuff," she commented.

Allie suddenly pointed out the window. "Look," she said, gesturing towards the mouth of the harbour. A row of big fishing boats was making its way through the entrance of the harbour, heading over to the brightly coloured sheds along the wharf. Outside the buildings, there were stacks of old weathered lobster traps, ready for sale to the tourists eager to take home a unique souvenir of their visit to the Island.

"They're bringing in a fresh catch of lobster," Christine told her friends. They heard Monica honking the horn and the girls started making their way back to the car.

"Can you sign our guest book before youse go?" Bud Gallant asked as the girls headed towards the door. He watched as they signed, and then he turned and looked at Christine in surprise.

"You're the lighthouse girl, aren't you?" Bud asked, turning the guest book around to get another look. "Aye, Christine Miller from Charlottetown, PEI. You helped to save the Governors Light. Well done, my girl."

Christine was too surprised to say anything. She just smiled at the bewhiskered lightkeeper and headed out to the car where her mother was waiting for them.

"The lighthouse girl," teased Brittany. "You certainly are the local celebrity now, aren't you?"

"That's amazing that he knew who you were," Allie added, shaking her head in surprise.

"It's a small place," Christine insisted, though secretly she was pleased that Bud Gallant had recognized her. She wished now that she had asked him questions about his lighthouse. She settled into the back seat with Allie, watching the coastline flying past as they made their way along the north shore towards Cavendish.

Monica insisted that they visit Green Gables. The girls were more interested in watching the Japanese tourists than actually paying attention to the tour about Lucy Maud Montgomery. They stared in amazement as the Japanese women walked through the house, some with tears flowing down their faces, taking pictures of every room, every piece of furniture.

"Almost everyone in Japan grows up reading *Anne of Green Gables*," Monica whispered to the girls. "For many of them, this is a lifelong dream, to visit Green Gables and some of the places Lucy Maud Montgomery describes in the book. Many Japanese couples even come here to get married, dozens of them every year."

The girls shook their heads in amazement. Christine smiled with pleasure at the thought of Prince Edward Island as a place where the dreams of these Japanese visitors came true. That only added to her growing conviction that there was, in fact, something magical about this place. She was too embarrassed to try to explain it out loud, but looking at her mother's face, she knew that her mother shared what she was feeling. Before they left Green Gables, Allie convinced Monica and Christine to pose for a picture outside the famous landmark, which seemed to please Mrs. Miller. Christine imagined that the photograph was something they would both treasure someday.

The girls spent the afternoon lazing around the Cavendish beach, while Monica visited the craft shops. On the way back to Charlottetown, they stopped at a roadside seafood spot and ate buns filled with lobster meat, as they watched the seadoos dashing in and out of the mussel lines in the harbour.

Rob Miller was waiting for them when they got home. He didn't mention a word about why he had been called in to work, but Christine heard her parents having a long conversation downstairs in the kitchen. She heard her mother cry out, at one point, but couldn't catch anything that they were saying. Christine scanned her parents' faces as they gathered in the hallway to leave for the lighthouse. Her mom and dad chatted with the girls from Ontario about their trip around the Island, as they waited for Scott and Jennifer to arrive.

Christine introduced her friends from Ontario to her friends from the Island. The young people were a little shy at first, but the girls soon loosened up as they loaded into the Jeep to make the trek to the lighthouse. Scott went in the car with Christine's dad, following the Jeep along the now-familiar route to the Governors Light.

On the way out to the lighthouse, Jennifer sat in the back seat with Brittany and Allie. They sat there enthralled, listening to Jennifer's history of the Governors Light. Occasionally, the Island girl would stop mid-sentence to point out a local landmark or a ripening crop of potatoes.

"I love it in the spring when the potato plants first appear," Jennifer told the Ontario girls. "They're so green against the red soil. It's my favourite time of the year."

"They're beautiful now," Brittany sighed contentedly, pointing to the fields of flowering potatoes.

Sitting in the front seat with her mom, Christine thought back to her own arrival on the Island. She had been so busy being miserable, she had missed the spectacular scenery.

Now the skyline of Toronto had faded in Christine's memory and this was the landscape that filled her dreams. "Home," she whispered to herself, and stared out the window.

Chapter Thirty-Three

LOST ... AND FOUND

*A*s the car pulled onto the final drive before the Governors Light, Monica turned to Jennifer and winked. "You will not only have the pleasure tonight of a tour of one of the Island's most popular tourist attractions," Christine's mom announced, with a smile. "There is also a very special guest here this evening, in honour of the visit of Brittany and Allie."

She wanted to ask her parents how they had arranged for this tour of the lighthouse, but just then the Old Salt came out the door. Christine was happy to see the old man was still living there. She noticed that a campfire had been started out in the picnic area.

"I'm just on my way to tell a ghost story or two once the sun goes down," the Old Salt said proudly. He noticed Christine's look of surprise. "Aye, the official storyteller I am now. Thanks again to yer mother and father."

Christine introduced her friends as the Old Salt gestured to the group to follow him over to the campfire. A group of lawn chairs had been arranged in a circle. Allie pushed a couple of chairs aside and rolled Brittany into the circle.

"I think we need a story to set the mood before you have the rest of your tour," the old sailor suggested.

"'Tis the sea that's the true star of all my stories," he said, settling into his storyteller's voice. The girls from Ontario exchanged delighted looks with Christine. She wondered if they could even make out what he was saying. Not that it really mattered. His accent and expressions were a big part of the Old Salt's charm, she thought.

"I'm just the, what do you call it … the spokesman for the sea. I speak for 'er, because she speaks to me," he continued.

"But some of the stories are so sad, so many people have died," Christine said to him. She had never had the courage to ask him about losing his brother and his nephews, but she had always wondered about them.

"Aye my dear, she's a cruel mistress and many families have paid a mighty price for living off her goodness," the Old Salt nodded. "But she's also a beauty and she stirs me heart still."

He paused for a moment, lost in thought, staring out across the waters of the Charlottetown Harbour. Just then, a Ford Explorer pulled into the driveway in front of the lighthouse and a tall, distinguished looking man climbed out. He walked over to join the group at the fire. He nodded at Rob and Monica Miller. The Old Salt seemed to know him too and gave him a friendly nod. The man settled into the chair and gestured for the Old Salt to continue. He smiled at Christine, too. She thought he looked familiar, but couldn't quite place him.

"You've heard of the Yankee Gale of 1851, which took near 100 ships," the Old Salt continued and most of his audience nodded. "Well, some twenty years later, there was another fierce gale. We call 'er the August Gale of 1873, and she too was a vicious one."

He unrolled a weathered map of Prince Edward Island and ran a tobacco-stained finger over the north end of the Island.

"Many ships were lost in the August Gale, but one of the most tragic stories was that of the FAITH. She and her crew were stranded as the storm began just outside of the Northport Harbour," he explained and indicated the exact location of the narrow opening of the harbour that was still used today.

"Why didn't they just get off the ship?" Jennifer asked and the Old Salt shook his head.

"They say that the tides rose by five feet and all the beaches were flooded. All the crew were likely lashed to the ship to keep from being washed overboard. They'd ne'er make it to shore, even as close as it was," he replied. "Some time that night, the ship lurched in the mountainous waves and the cargo came smashing through the hull. You see, she was carrying steel rails. They smashed her hull to pieces."

Christine imagined the sheer force of the steel smashing through the fragile hull of the ship, the only thing that stood between the crew and the ravenous waters.

"Then one of the masts broke clean away. It was swept away, crew and all," he concluded, sadly. "For days after the storm, bodies washed up on the shore from North Cape to Cascumpec. All the crew and the FAITH itself were lost."

The Old Salt picked up the guitar out of its case, which he had brought with him from the lighthouse. He softly strummed what sounded like an old hymn. He started to sing in a husky voice. Christine looked over where Brittany and Allie were sitting. All through the Old Salt's story, the two girls had strained forward as if they didn't want to miss a word. Now they watched in wonder as the old man began to sing.

Let the lower lights be burning,
Send a beam across the wave,
Some poor aching, struggling seaman
You may rescue, you may save.

Dark the night of sin has fallen
loud the angry billows roar,
Eager eyes are watching, longing,
for the lights along the shore.

Trim your feeble lamps, my brothers,
some poor sailor's tempest tossed,
Trying now to make the harbour
in the darkness may be lost.

Everyone sat in silence as the last chord of the guitar echoed around them and the only sound was a light wind whistling up from the shore. The sun was starting to dip on the horizon and Christine felt a slight chill pass through the circle, even though it was still very warm.

The Old Salt got up from his chair, and Marco Polo jumped up too. "Well, I won't be holdin' you back from yer tour no longer," he said. "I've got me people waitin' for a story a while later and ye're welcome to join us. A night of story-tellin' lies ahead." He gave Christine a playful tap on the arm as he headed over to the reception building. "You've done 'em all proud, my girl," he said. Christine beamed with pleasure, though she wasn't quite sure what he meant. She noticed that he also stopped to shake hands with the mysterious man who had joined their circle.

"I'll be right with you," Rob said, standing with the Old Salt. "We've just a couple of papers for Mr. Bernard to sign."

"Oh, enough of this Mr. Bernard business," the Old Salt chuckled. "You make me sound like some kind of corporate tycoon. The Old Salt is me name."

Everyone laughed. Jennifer and Christine walked over to the cliff as the others stood around the fire waiting for the Old Salt to lead them over to the lighthouse.

"The tide's going out now," Jennifer pointed to one of the buoys. She showed Christine how to look for the trail of water going by. "And the wind's coming from the south, going right against it. That's why the waves are so big."

They turned and looked up at the Governors Light. The red and white paint made the tower look even taller than before the renovations.

"It sure has changed since the first time we came out to visit," Jennifer said. "This has become a piece of Island history now."

"But I will still never be an Islander," Christine replied. Scott and Jennifer teased her because, according to local tradition, you were only an Islander if you were born on PEI.

"True, but I bet your children will be." Jennifer giggled and Christine blushed, but she hoped her friend was right.

Scott joined them at the cliff. "The sun's going down, so we should get them up to the balcony." The girls nodded. Jennifer left them for a moment, staring out at the harbour.

"I've made a deal with my dad," Scott told Christine, his eyes glued to a fishing boat making its way into the marina at Peakes Quay. "I'll fish with Doug in exchange for tuition money when it comes time to go to university."

"And he agreed?" Christine asked, thrilled for her boyfriend.

Scott shrugged. "He's still not happy about it, but he understands that it's important to me. He wanted both of us to go into the business. But at least he'll have Doug."

"So, you'll be leaving the Island too?" Christine said, sadly, thinking about Jennifer's plans to go away to university.

"Yes, but you know what? An Islander always comes back. You'll learn that for yourself," Scott replied, taking Christine's hand and giving it a gentle squeeze. Hand in hand, they walked up to the lighthouse.

Monica was standing at the doorway with Christine's friends. "It's the most beautiful sunset you will ever experience," she told them confidently. Then, turning to Christine, she added. "But first we have a surprise."

Monica flung open the door and Betty McIntosh came to the doorway.

Christine glanced at her mother with surprise. Then she rushed up the steps and gave the frail, elderly woman a hug.

"I'm so happy you could be here to meet my friends," Christine murmured. She brushed away a tiny tear that welled up as she thought about the first time she had met the old couple, here at the lighthouse.

"You've done a lovely job, my dear," Betty whispered, her voice husky with emotion. "The lighthouse looks as good as new. And the cottages are lovely. It means so much to know that other people are going to have a chance to share this beautiful spot."

Christine was struck by the older woman's comment. She had never thought of it that way. Betty was right. It didn't matter who owned the place. The important thing was that the lighthouse had been saved, and now other people would have a chance to look at it, even if it was from a distance.

As she took the old woman's arm and went inside the lighthouse, Christine caught her breath. All around the floor, there were boxes and boxes of lighthouse memorabilia. It was all of Mack's collection.

In one corner, the giant light of etched glass sat on a red and white podium and the setting sun shining through the windows of the lighthouse made its fine edges sparkle. The walls were already covered in gigantic photographs of the other lighthouses from across the Island. Pieces of old rigging and brightly painted wooden buoys had been hung from the rafters. An old wheel from an ancient shipwreck had been retrieved and mounted, as if it was ready for eager visitors who wanted to try their hand at navigation.

"It's incredible," Christine whispered. She looked over at Jennifer. Her friend was as shocked as she was. Scott gave a low whistle. "This'll have the tourists talking," he said.

Betty looked around her old familiar home and gave the teenagers a smile, a look of pride and pleasure written across her face. "It's a fine, fine thing you've done," she said to all of them. "You've done Mack proud."

Christine turned to her mother. "How …"

Rob Miller came in the door, followed by the man from the campfire. "This is my boss, Ray MacPherson. He has generously offered a donation of money to get the lighthouse museum up and running. And he is also the new owner of the cottages."

Now Christine realized where she had seen Mr. MacPherson before. He had been part of the group staying at the cottages when they came out to visit the Old Salt a few weeks ago.

"I was here for our company workshop," Mr. MacPherson explained, stepping forward to shake hands with Betty McIntosh, who gave him a tearful pat on the arm. "My father was a lobster fisher and his father before him. In fact, they were old friends of Walter Bernard. The Old Salt, I guess you call him. When Rob told me what was going on with the lighthouse, I wanted to help out. I was out of the country on business and only got back this weekend. It has taken us a day of wheelin' and dealin', but I think we've got it all ironed out now. So the heritage society will get its lighthouse museum and the company gets a fine investment in these cottages. Sounds like a good deal, all round."

Everyone shook hands in a flurry of congratulations. Brittany and Allie looked slightly confused. "I'll explain it all later," Christine whispered.

"Hey, we're going to miss the sunset," Jennifer said, pointing out the window. She headed up the stairs and opened the trapdoor, leading to the platform around the light. Christine's parents went up, along with Ray MacPherson.

Brittany looked nervously up at the platform. Christine realized that her friend had probably overdone it today, trying hard not to use her cane or her wheelchair as they toured around the Island. That was just like Brittany, Christine thought. Still, she was determined that her friend was going to experience the magic of the light.

"Brittany, it's not that high. Really," Christine insisted.

"I'm just not sure I can get up there," Brittany replied, apologetically, giving them a wave of her cane.

"That's why I'm here," Scott jumped in. "In addition to my dazzling personality and good looks. I'm also extremely strong." He flexed his muscles, and Christine elbowed him in the stomach teasingly. She looked over at Brittany, willing her friend to accept his offer.

Brittany gazed up at the trapdoor and then at her friends, who nodded encouragingly. But she still wasn't convinced.

"Believe me, you will not want to miss this sunset," Scott cajoled her.

Brittany took a deep breath and pulled herself out of the chair. She hobbled over to the steps, and then blushed a deep red as Scott carefully swept her up into his arms. Christine and Allie followed along close behind as they headed up the steep stairs to the balcony of the lighthouse.

"Why is it that you found this charming attractive guy and I ended up with a jerk?" Brittany shouted teasingly to Christine. It was Scott's turn to blush.

"Don't answer that," Brittany added quickly. "And besides I finally ditched the jerk once and for all." A cloud seemed to pass over Brittany's face, but it lifted as soon as they passed through the open hatch. A burst of light swept over her face as the girls and Scott emerged out onto the balcony.

Christine felt a surge of happiness as she watched her friends from Ontario ooh-ing and aah-ing with amazement as they gazed up at the magnificent flashing light. Christine stepped carefully towards the railing, closing her eyes to feel the warm wind of the setting day. When she opened them, she gasped. Over in a corner of the balcony, wrapped in a heavy sweater and blankets, was Mack, with Betty watching over him like a hawk. Mack lifted his good arm and gave Christine a wave, and his eyes glinted with pleasure. Christine ran over and hugged the old man.

"You're the special guest," she sputtered. She hugged him again. Then she introduced Allie and Brittany.

Scott carefully placed Brittany in a chair that had been set up next to Mack. Brittany carefully reached over and took the old man's hand. "You were the reason I came to PEI," she whispered. "You and your lighthouse kept me going ..." Her voice faded off into the warm evening wind.

"Look," Scott shouted from around the other side of the light. The girls all turned their attention back to the setting sun, which had just fallen below the horizon of trees and red clay cliffs. It was as if someone had lit a match and set the entire sky ablaze. Waves of orange, red and yellow danced above the fluttering white sails of a group of boats just making their way back into the harbour.

Everyone watched in silence, lost in their own thoughts.

"This is one of those perfect moments in life," Christine whispered to Scott, who now stood beside her. He nodded, his gaze still on the fiery sky.

Betty finally broke the contented silence. "Dave, it's time to go," she said in a gentle voice.

"Can we have just one more minute?" Brittany begged. She was still holding the old man's hand. Mack's eyes pleaded with his wife, and Betty nodded.

"I'm going to run down and get my camera. This is such a great picture," Christine said quietly to her friend.

"I don't need a picture," Brittany whispered. "I'll always remember this moment." Her eyes were riveted on the glorious colours all around her and a look of total calm came across her face. Christine could never remember her friend looking as relaxed, or as beautiful, as she did at that moment.

As she made her way down the winding stairs and out to the car, Christine pondered her friend's words. What was it that made this lighthouse so special? Christine thought back to the first time she had seen it, looking across the harbour from Victoria Park. That now seemed like such a long time ago. So much had changed since then.

Christine walked past the stack of boxes on the main floor and noticed an old life ring. It had been used many years ago to pull a drowning sailor out of the harbour. She shivered at the thought of the lives lost — and saved — because of the lighthouse.

And then it hit her. That was what made the lighthouse so magical. She looked up at Brittany and Mack, now two silhouettes against the throbbing light. Both of them had been through great trials over the last year, and both had survived. And somehow, for both of them, the lighthouse had been their life ring.

Christine smiled to herself and whispered "Thank you" to the light. She raised her hand to her heart, the way Mack had earlier that summer. Christine understood now what he meant, and what the lighthouse meant. In one way or another, the lighthouse had saved them all.

AUTHOR'S NOTE

The Governors Lighthouse does not exist: it is a composite of several existing PEI lighthouses. There is a Governors Island that suggested the name for the lighthouse in the novel. The Blockhouse Light sits at the entrance of the Charlottetown Harbour and was my inspiration for the Governors Light. For more information about the history of the Governors Island, I recommend *Geographical Names of Prince Edward Island* by Alan Rayburn (Ottawa: Canadian Permanent Committee on Geographical Names, 1973).

I consulted several books for information and inspiration for the songs and historical passages found in the novel. Especially helpful were: *Shipwrecks and Seafaring Tales of Prince Edward Island* by Julie Watson (Halifax: Nimbus, 1993) and *Against Darkness and Storm: Lighthouses of the Northeast* by Harry Thurston (Halifax: Nimbus, 1993).

The song "Heart of Oak" was written by David Garrick in 1759. The version I have used here appeared in the *Burl Ives Songbook* (1953). The hymn "Let the lower lights be burning" was written by P.P. Bliss and appeared in the *Broadman Hymnal* (Nashville, TN: 1940).

ALSO FROM RAGWEED PRESS

The Twisting Road Tea Room
Deb Loughead

> *"The little girl could have been me, about six years ago.*
> *Long spindly legs, sallow skin, heart-shaped face, chubby*
> *cheeks, mousy hair. But it was the sight of him that made*
> *me crank my neck around in an unnatural way, then shriek*
> *in anguish like I'd just been stabbed. It was the sight of him*
> *that made me lose control of my mountain bike and crash*
> *full-tilt into the back of a parked car. Fade to black ..."*

Maggie's father has recently died and Maggie and her mother are having a hard time coping with their grief and making ends meet living in a big city. Out of the blue, Maggie's mother inherits a house in Nova Scotia. She is convinced that moving there will give them a new start. Maggie isn't so sure, especially when they arrive to find that they must share their new home with a stranger. The house's history, which includes a mysterious presence, reveals secrets and adventures that make life in a small town surprisingly exciting.

Toronto author Deb Loughead has one book to her credit, *All I Need and Other Poems* (Moonstruck Press, 1998). Although she has never lived in Nova Scotia, she visits there whenever she can.

ISBN 0-921556-79-9 $8.95

Ragweed Press books are available in quality bookstore everywhere. Ask for our books at your favourite bookstore. Phone (902-566-5750), fax (902-566-4473) or send us an email (books@ragweed.com) to receive our free catalogue. As well, you can visit us online at our website: www.Ragweed.com. We also accept individual prepaid orders sent to: Ragweed Press, P.O. Box 2023, Charlottetown, PEI, Canada, C1A 7N7. Please add postage and handling ($3.00 for first book and $1.00 for each additional book) to your order. Canadian residents add 7% GST to total amount. GST registration number R104383120. Prices are subject to change without notice.